AN UNFORGETTABLE MOMENT

DARA GIRARD

ISBN: 978-1949764383

AN UNFORGETTABLE MOMENT

Published by ILORI Press Books

This is a work of fiction. Names, characters, places and incidents are either the product of the author's imagination or are used fictitiously, and any resemblance to actual persons, living or dead is entirely coincidental.

ILORI PRESS BOOKS, LLC

P.O. Box 10332

Silver Spring, MD 20914

www.iloripressbooks.com

Duvall Sisters

The Glass Slipper Project

Taming Mariella

A Reluctant Hero

The Black Stockings Society

Power Play

A Gentleman's Offer

Body Chemistry

Round the Clock

Return of the Black Stockings Society

Playing for Keeps

After Hours

A Private Affair

Just One Look

Private Lessons

Ladies of the Pen

Words of Seduction

Pages of Passion

Beneath the Covers

Henson Series

Table for Two

Gaining Interest

Careless Rapture

Dangerous Curves

Familiar Stranger

It Happened One Wedding

Unexpected Pleasure

Midnight Promise

Sweet Temptation

Always and Forever

Truly Yours

Say Yes

Clifton Sisters

The Sapphire Pendant

The Amber Stone

The Emerald Ring

Fortune Brothers

A Tempting Proposal

A Seductive Arrangement

Novels

Honest Betrayal

The Daughters of Winston Barnett

Remember My Name

Illusive Flame

Winterwood Lane

Promise Me

AN UNFORGETTABLE MOMENT

Dara Girard

He'd never been so scared in his life.

He wasn't afraid of the dark like his younger sister, Gisele, he was really proud of that. Even when his babysitter thought he was asleep, he'd snuck back into the movie room, what his mother liked to call the 'theater' room, and watched the scary movie that had her gasping. He didn't even jump once or even have a nightmare. He'd thought the monster was fun. He was still too small to go on some fair rides, but he was certain that when he was allowed on his first roller coaster he wouldn't scream once. No, being scared wasn't his thing.

Until now.

Now at eight years old he faced something that made his throat dry, his skin tingle, his heart race. But he couldn't let his father know that. He didn't want to disappoint him. His father had told him this morning that he was taking him on a drive. It was rare that his father had time to take him anywhere. His father was usually too busy with work to take him to soccer practice or pick him up from school or remember his birthday. But he respected him. His father was a man who gained respect.

He hoped to be like him some day, even though there were already whispers that he was falling short, 'both figuratively and literally', he'd overheard an aunt say, whatever that meant. He was small for his age and hadn't achieved anything remarkable yet. He wasn't the brightest in his class or very athletic and he was too shy to be popular, although he did have some friends. But not like his father. His father could charm anyone; people swarmed around him like bees protecting their queen, when he entered a room. One day when he'd learned about different careers in school, he'd asked his father what he did. His father just looked at him and said 'survive'. He still didn't know what that meant. His other friend's Dads owned banks, ran companies, owned apartments, even the cleaning lady was easier to understand when she told him that her daughter was a police officer and her son a baker.

His father remained a mystery. From his mother he heard that his father owned and managed properties and that he would do the same one day. But he didn't know exactly what that meant.

But one day seemed so far away. He wanted to know more now. But he felt that his father didn't trust him yet, that he had more to prove. And soon he would. He was studying harder and running up and down the stairs when no one was looking so that he could be stronger and he was eating his vegetables like their chef told him so that he could be taller. He really hoped to grow more. One day he would make his father proud.

For now he would do whatever his father told him to do.

So that chilly spring morning, when the dew was ripe on the manicured lawn and bushes, he didn't ask questions when his Dad took him to one of their cars—the black one with the silver trim, although he preferred the one his mother liked to drive (it was bright green with soft seats). He buckled his seatbelt as if he were getting buckled into a carnival ride. His heart raced, but he hoped his feelings didn't show. That was one thing he'd learned early, Duchamps didn't show their feelings. That showed weakness. He may be small, but he couldn't be weak.

It was a long drive and he wished his father had let him take a game along, but when he mentioned this regret, his father said, "Your mind is your greatest weapon, use it." Max made sure to never say he was bored. Ever. His father let him know that only stupid people found life boring. Winners always found something to do. So Max sighed as he watched the landscape outside his window leave the comfortable greenery of his neighborhood to the paved roads of the highway bracketed by large trees which slowly gave way to flat valleys with brown horses and black and white cows. Then more trees, a large industrial building that spat out dark smoke and a smell that had him covering his nose. He saw some more concrete buildings and strip malls.

Finally after what seemed like *forever,* his father turned off the highway and there were large trees again and spotted in-between were houses that looked like square toy boxes. One after the other. If he hadn't seen a kid riding a bicycle he wouldn't have imagined anyone living there. It was a strange neighborhood. Why were there piles of trash lining the street? He saw a cola can bouncing along the sidewalk and a plastic bag blowing in the branches of a skinny tree like a lost kite.

"Are we in Florida now?"

His father snorted amused. "Why would you think that?"

"Because of the boarded up buildings. I see them on the windows. Was there a storm?" On TV he'd seen people protecting their homes that way when a hurricane was about to hit.

"No, we're not in Florida. I thought you were paying attention."

"Attention?"

"To the signs. We've gone through two states."

He felt bad. He hadn't seen the signs. He hated how his father could say things that made him feel stupid. He glanced around and saw a car with a license plate and hazarded a guess. "We're in South Carolina."

"That's right."

Whoa, why had they driven all the way from Virginia to here?

He bit his lip as the car turned onto a dirt road and then stopped.

He opened his mouth to ask, "Why are we stopping?"

but quickly stopped himself. Because he didn't want to annoy his father and he didn't want any sign of fear to be heard in his voice. He didn't want to be in a place like this.

He remembered seeing a place like this once on TV; there had been a fire or something and he remembered seeing a child crying and a woman looking sad. He'd stood there transfixed before his mother switched the station. He tried to ask her about what he had seen, but she told him that he'd learn more when he was older.

He must be older now, he thought as he walked behind his father up the makeshift driveway, which was dusty and filled with holes, towards the house that reminded Max of a blind monster. It had a wide open mouth where a door should have been, and two black, empty eyes where windows had probably once been but had been replaced with black sheets. Max swallowed as he followed his father up the crooked front porch steps. He'd rather be at home playing in his yard. He didn't know why his father wanted to go into this empty house.

Once they stepped inside the house, he took his Dad's hand, half afraid his father would pull away and be angry with him. But he didn't. His father didn't look at him as he walked down the dark hall, and Max felt as if he were walking inside the monster's throat. His father gave Max's hand a slight squeeze of reassurance; Max's heart didn't stop racing, but he felt a little more at ease. He smelled the faint odor of fried chicken and beer. He remembered the smell of beer from a distant cousin, with a loud laugh who'd only visited once and never again.

Max listened to insects buzzing, before he heard the sound of voices. Someone was here!

They walked into the front room and Max stiffened when he saw an old man sitting on a worn green couch in front of a TV. The man reminded him of a walking stick he'd once seen in a book on insects. He was the same brown color, skinny, shirtless and looked like he hadn't shaved in days. Although he looked dirty, the place smelled clean and then he noticed the orange candle burning in the room.

"Dad, I brought someone to meet you," his father said.

Max looked up at his father alarmed. Dad? This skinny, little old man was his *grandfather*? He'd never seen a picture of him. His father never spoke about his family. He knew everyone was a kid once, but he always had a hard time thinking of his Dad as one. He was too grown up. Too big. A 'self-made' man was what his mother always called him. Max knew more about her side, her sister, two brothers and parents, than his father's.

But now he could see why his father hadn't mentioned this man. There wasn't much to say.

The old man didn't look at them. He kept his gaze on the TV screen. Max followed his gaze and heard a gunshot before he saw a man and the horse he was riding fall down. He didn't like Westerns very much, but was glad to see the horse get up and ride away. He liked animals. He understood them a little better than people.

"This is my son Maximillian," his father said. Max inwardly cringed. He hated when anyone used his full name. "I just wanted you to know." His father put some money on top of the TV.

"I've got a sister too," Max said. He didn't know why he said it and the quick, tight squeeze his father gave his hand was far from reassuring. It was a warning. It told him to be quiet. But Max was proud of his little sister who'd just turned three and didn't know why his father had forgotten to mention her. He didn't care how scary this old man was he should know the truth.

The old man, Max was still too scared to consider him family, let alone his grandfather, shifted his dark gaze away from the TV screen and pinned them on Max. He then lifted his gaze to his father's face and a slow smile touched his lips. "You think this visit will change things?"

"I know it will."

He looked at Max again and motioned him forward. He then whispered something that Max didn't completely understand but made him shiver. He wasn't sure whether it was the old man's words or tone that affected him the most. He then sat back in his chair and said in a regular tone, "Come visit anytime." He looked back at the TV.

When they left the house, Max took a deep breath. He scrambled into the backseat and put on his seatbelt, struggling to make sure it didn't cut him off at the neck. Whenever he was with his mother she kept putting him in a special car seat which was really embarrassing. She said when he grew a little more she'd get rid of it, but he wasn't growing fast enough and hated that he had to ride in a baby seat like his sister (they called it a car seat but they couldn't fool him). He was five years older than her.

His father turned around from the driver's seat and looked at him. "Were you scared?"

Max swallowed hard. He wanted to prove he was brave; he wanted to show that nothing could scare him, but he didn't want to lie. Especially when he knew his father knew the truth. Everyone knew the truth. Few things could scare Max except his father. His father frightened him in ways he couldn't understand. As much as the house and the old man scared him, the thought of being caught in a lie scared him even more. He nodded ashamed.

His father's tone tightened. "When I talk to you, I expect to hear a reply."

"I was," Max said.

"You were what?"

"Scared." He inwardly cringed. He hated that his voice shook.

"Really scared?" his father pressed.

He nodded again then quickly remembered to say, "Yes," when his father narrowed his eyes.

His father nodded satisfied. "Good. I wanted to bring you here to show you where we come from." He pointed to the house. "But this is not who we are. Anytime you slip, anytime you fall remember that this is where you could end up. But you follow my lead, you trust my words without question, and I'll make sure you never do. Understand?"

Max swallowed. "Yes."

"What did he whisper to you?"

Max told him and his father laughed. A cruel laugh. "There's your proof. The man's a fool."

His father turned the car around and headed down the driveway. And Max didn't look back even though he had a strange sense that the old man in the monster house was watching. The words he'd whispered to Max following him, but he wouldn't fully understand their meaning until it was nearly too late.

CHAPTER 2

"You have a sister."

That was the last thing Desiree Foster expected to hear as she finished off her mother's banana pudding. The hospital food was surprisingly good and she'd missed dinner. She hadn't been able to eat after worrying about her mother all day. Her mother had been rushed to the hospital in a dazed state and was only hours away from being sent to the psych ward when an insistent ER doctor noticed the real cause of her mother's symptoms and discovered she'd had a major adverse reaction to her new allergy medicine (a prescribed medication Desiree could barely pronounce which was probably why she was the unemployed jane-of-all-trades while her brother was the one who'd studied mechatronics). It had conflicted with her high blood pressure and anti-anxiety medicine.

Nearly getting one's mother admitted as psychotic

was more than enough shock for the month and now possibly her mother was hallucinating again? Did she need to call a doctor?

"Don't look at me like that," her mother said.

How else could she look at her? Her mother had never mentioned that she'd had other children besides herself and her younger brother, Laurence.

Desiree set her spoon down on the bed tray and stood to adjust her mother's pillow. It was a habit she'd gotten used to. It wasn't the first time her mother had been admitted to the hospital. "Maybe you should rest."

"I saw her on the TV."

Yes, she was definitely hallucinating. Desiree looked around for the call button so she could alert a nurse.

Her mother grabbed her arm. "I don't need to rest and I'm not crazy. I know what I'm saying. I know what I saw. " Her voice sounded urgent. "He stole her away from me."

Desiree had heard her mother's tone in many different ways—frightened, anxious, worried—but never this insistent. In spite of herself she knew she had to listen. "Who stole what?"

"Walter. My first husband. He stole my precious daughter from me."

Desiree blinked, looking at the face of the woman she'd called 'mother' for almost thirty-one years, as if she were a stranger. "You never told us you'd been married before."

"It was something I wanted to forget. I haven't seen my dear Amelia since she was three years old. I'd searched for her for more than twenty years, even when we moved to Michigan before returning back here, then gave up." She pointed to the TV fastened on the wall. "Until I saw her on there."

"Mom," Desiree said gently. "If it's been that long, how can you know it's her? You last saw her when she was three and she's a grown woman now and—"

Her mother's grip tightened on her arm. "I saw her face. I know it's her. She has some of Walter's features. And Walter's face is one I'll never forget. That man stole so much from me." She held Desiree's arm until it started to hurt. "I need you to help me. Before I die I want to hold her in my arms and hear her voice again."

"Mom," Desiree said, loosening her mother's hold, "you're only in your sixties. You're not going to die soon."

"When you reach my age, every moment is precious. You start to think about time that gets wasted. I don't want to lose this chance. She's changed her name, but now I have something to go on. You can look her up and get her to come and see me."

Desiree sat down and sighed. She tried to get a handle of her racing thoughts. A half-sister? Her mother had been married before? Her mother wanted her to find some woman she'd seen on TV? She softened her voice not wanting to upset her mother any more. Her mother had a fragile constitution although by looking at her one wouldn't think so. She was a sturdily built woman with two gray braids pulled behind into a bun at the base of her neck. Big, brown eyes that always looked lost and a full mouth that rarely smiled.

Desiree had an urge to grab her cell phone and text something to Million, the one person who'd kept her sane these past several years. Someone, ironically, who had also changed her life in a hospital setting like this, five years ago.

ive years ago

She was doing her rounds as a patient service representative (a job she'd loved and would eventually lose due to budget cuts) on the VIP ward of the hospital when she heard crying. Desiree peeked inside the room and saw a young black woman in a hospital bed, surrounded by flowers, her hands over her face.

"Are you hurting?" she asked her, cautiously entering the large suite. "Do you want me to get a nurse?"

"No," came the miserable reply.

"What's your name?"

The young woman hesitated then said in barely a whisper, "Felice."

"Is there anything I can do for you, Felice?"

The young woman lowered her hands and looked at her. "Make me pretty again."

Desiree stared at the young woman confused. She

was more than pretty enough with warm brown skin, long, dark lashes and eyebrows, and cupid bow lips. "From what I see you're beautiful."

Her lower lip trembled. "Not like before." She opened the front of her hospital gown and revealed a large bandage over her chest, one breast looked decidedly flatter than the other one.

Desiree walked over to her and stopped at the side of the bed. "Breast cancer is scary and you've been though a lot, but at least you're alive."

Felice shook her head. "It wasn't cancer. Maybe that's what I'll tell people. I can never have a boyfriend looking like this." Tears gathered again.

"You will find someone who will accept you."

"I only did it to be like her. She said men like women with bigger chests and my Dad wouldn't listen and neither would my brother and he usually understands everything, but he wouldn't help so..." She released a shaky sigh. "She said she wanted to do something nice for me so that she could win back my brother's trust after breaking his heart by leaving him. She promised me it would be okay. I'd be safe. That the doctor was the best around. That it'd be a quick trip to Mexico, a one night stay and then I'd be back with a better figure. But when I got there it was so awful. I wanted to call my brother, but I was afraid he'd be so mad at me for listening to her. Then after the surgery, when I came back, I felt so ill and it started bleeding. Now I'm deformed and I wish I were dead."

"Okay."

"Okay?"

Desiree nodded, although she wasn't sure of what she'd just heard. "You're hurting, this is awful, you have every right to how you feel right now. But know that you're loved. Know that you survived for a reason and that you'll get past this pain. But if the pain is too deep I understand and will leave you alone."

"You sound like my brother," Felice muttered annoyed.

"It must have been harder for him to say, because he'd miss you. Since I don't know you, I wouldn't."

"You don't understand."

"What hurts the most? The embarrassment? The betrayal of the doctor? Your friend? That you lied to your family? The surgery? I'm not saying it's fair, but life isn't fair. I'm not saying that your pain and hurt isn't real. But just know that the pain won't last forever, even though right now it feels that way."

She mumbled something.

Desiree leaned closer. "What?"

"The pain *is* forever."

"Why would you think that?"

"Because I don't remember the last time I was very happy. My brother's even worse. Even if I wanted to end my life, I couldn't because of him. If I weren't here, he wouldn't..." Her words fell away.

Desiree understood. She had the same bond with her brother. "Your lost would devastate him."

"I made life worse for him already. Our father blames him because he's the eldest and he was supposed to look after me, like I'm some kid. It hurts more to know the awful things Dad said to him. I haven't been able to talk to him yet."

Desiree pulled up a chair and sat "Tell me about him."

Felice looked terrified. "You want me to talk about my father?"

"No, your brother." He seemed to be the one topic that made her eyes light up a bit.

As she'd hoped, Felice's face lost some of its sadness and she smiled. "Oh, he's the best in the world. You wouldn't think so to look at him, but he's the kindest most generous guy you could ever know. He's smart. He's good looking. He knows Brazilian jiu-jitsu, started two companies before the age of twenty-one, likes to go hiking and swimming. He's brave. He does his best to protect me—when I let him—and he's a got a little dog he calls AP."

"AP?"

"Yes, for 'abandoned puppy'. He rescued it. We'd been driving on the highway and we saw some jerk in a Jag toss something out the window into the woods. My brother had a bad feeling so he drove to the shoulder of the road, hopped out of the car and found the bag."

"And saw the dog inside," Desiree guessed.

"Yep, barely two years old we found out when we took him to the vet. My brother adopted him and called him AP."

"So your brother saves dogs, protects you, runs companies, is good looking and physically fit?"

"Yes."

"He sounds perfect," Desiree teased, certain Felice

had embellished a lot. No man could be that great. "Is he married?"

Felice laughed then her happy expression slowly faded away. "He was engaged, but...I don't think he'll ever marry now."

"There's plenty of time. There will be someone out there to change his mind."

She studied her. "Are you single?"

"I've got a boyfriend." And even if she were single, a guy like the one Felice had described sounded intimidating.

Felice lowered her eyes disappointed. "Oh."

Desiree didn't want her sinking into sadness again. She'd gotten her briefly laughing and smiling and she knew that was good for healing. "But here's what we're going to do. Think of this as part of your recovery. You're going to write your brother a letter. We won't send it, but it will be something that you can use to express yourself and get all your feelings out. Let him know how guilty you feel, talk about your father, anything."

Felice bit her lip. "I'm scared to." She hesitated. "And it hurts to write."

"That's okay." Desiree pulled out her notepad and a pen. "Dictate it to me. This will just be between us."

"Okay," Felice said then began, "Dear Million."

"Million?"

"Yes, that's what I call him. It's my little joke. He likes to make millions, plus, to me, he's one in a million."

"That's sweet."

A tiny grin touched her lips. "It also bugs him."

"You are a naughty sister."

"He loves me anyway."

"Of course, Okay, what do you want to say next?"

Felice sighed then said, "I've never known how to say this, but I'm sorry Mom hit you instead of me..." Desiree kept her eyes on the paper even though her hand slightly trembled as she wrote the words. She hadn't expected that and as Desiree wrote down more of Felice's words revealing all that the brother and sister had gone through together, she not only felt closer to Felice, but also her brother too.

Her brother sounded like an amazing person who had gone through a lot. She admired this stranger who had managed to keep his sister safe in a house that appeared so cold and withdrawn with two parents who seemed like distant relatives. She understood being under a parent you couldn't reach emotionally. While she didn't fear her mother, she feared her mother's moods. The ones that would cover the house in darkness and depression like a suffocating blanket. When she couldn't reach her or encourage her to come out of her room. When she felt like a stranger.

Felice rested her head back. "And that's it. Now I'm tired."

Desiree folded up the letter and tucked it inside a high end fashion magazine Felice had asked her to hide it in, which sat on the side table. "You did great."

"C-could you stay until I fall asleep?"

Desiree studied her face. From her expression she knew she would be fast asleep within seconds. "Okay."

She adjusted Felice's pillow then the sheets and sat back in her chair. She watched Felice close her eyes then stood and roamed the room. She bent down and smelled a bouquet of pink roses that sat on the windowsill, then noticed the card tucked inside. It had one word: My. She frowned thinking that was strange until she looked at another bouquet and saw another note and the word: foolish and then a third bouquet, with a note that said: Felice.

By then she'd noticed the pattern and knew all the cards were from the same person. She gathered them together then got some scotch tape from the nurses' station and put them together on Felice's bed so she could see them when she woke up. The full message said: My foolish Felice. I will always love you no matter what. Million.

Such a sweet gesture touched Desiree to the core. What a wonderful, caring brother. She glanced at the glossy magazine where she'd hid Felice's letter. She wanted to write this amazing man a letter too, but it wasn't something she wanted to hide. She'd put it on the tray and hoped Felice would share it.

Desiree sat down, flexed her fingers then began to write,

Dear Mill... She stopped. She couldn't call him Million. That was his sister's special name for him and since she said it annoyed him Desiree didn't want to do the same. She started again. *Dear M,*

I'll admit to being half in love with you. But don't worry, I'm not crazy. I'm just impressed by all that your sister shared about you. If you don't know this already, know that Felice loves you and that you're an amazing brother, friend and confidant. A son your parents can be proud of even if they don't show it. You can't change the world or how others are treated, but you managed to make her feel special and cared for. That's a gift not many people are willing to give even in families.

I guess I really wanted to write this so that you know you're not alone. I know it can feel that way. I wish I had someone like you to share the burden when a parent falters and lets you down. I have to be my little brother's rock and it hasn't always been easy. I know he doesn't adore me as much as your sister adores you, but that's okay.

I wish I had your courage to stand up and fight when something was wrong, but I like to smooth things over rather than confront them. She's lucky to have someone like you in her life. I wish I had a chance to meet you. But know that there will be days that I'm thinking of you and wishing you well.

Sincerely,

A friend

She folded the letter and wrote, *For your brother M,* and left it on Felice's lap for her to see when she woke up.

Desiree thought of that letter five years later surprised by her impulsiveness. It was rare for her to bare herself to anyone like that, but somehow writing to a stranger and not signing her name felt both bold and safe. She wondered if he had read it, if it reached his heart as she hoped it would or did he find it too sentimental and throw it away.

She hoped Felice had completely healed and gotten the reconstruction surgery she needed. Brothers and sisters. Family. And now hers may be expanding with someone who'd been featured on television.

Desiree patted her mother's hand as she would a distressed child. "Reconnecting with her is not going to be that simple." When her mother looked upset, Desiree quickly said, "What's her name?"

"She was Amelia Breemer, but she's now called Ava Hughes Fortune."

CHAPTER 4

It was like living with a ghost.

It had been more than a year and she never talked about her mother. James Fortune looked over at his wife Ava as she sat in the great room, reading one of her favorite mangas, smiling to herself as she turned the page. He sat across from her working on his laptop, but unable to focus. The coming of summer always had him thinking about the past. About their wedding, about the passing of his mother.

Ava always let him reminisce about his mother, her garden, her smile, but one topic they never talked about was her life. Her father's betrayal, the fact that her mother had been looking for her but that his stepfather, Edgar, who her mother had worked for, had lost contact. When they'd first discovered the truth, that she'd been raised in Canada under a new name and identity, he'd been ready to start a search, but Ava kept delaying it so he didn't press her, but as more time passed he wondered what she was afraid of.

He knew her past was a delicate topic, but he'd grown tired of dancing around it. The silence was starting to hurt. He glanced at the cover of the manga, something called *Assassination Classroom* with some yellow faced monster on the cover. He couldn't understand his wife's fascination with the stories. Usually he waited until she finished, but this series seemed to last long, she'd already gone through a bunch of books, and he was getting restless. "We need to get started searching for her."

Ava turned a page and said with little interest, "Searching for whom?"

"Your mother."

She paused, before she turned another page. "What's the rush?"

"Time isn't on our side. We don't know how long this could take."

"I'm sure with Edgar's contacts it shouldn't take long," she said bored.

"Then let's do it."

"Later."

He sighed. "You always say that."

"Because I mean it."

He stood, reached over and snatched the manga from her. "I thought this was important to you."

She jumped to her feet, alarmed. "Don't lose my page!"

"You can always find it again."

"I'm at a crucial place. I'm about to find out if the students defeat the Reaper."

James looked at the following pages and quickly skimmed it. "I can easily tell you that. They—"

She covered his mouth, narrowed her eyes and said in a low voice, "Do you want to die?" She yanked the book from him and sat back down to continue reading.

He took the book back, grabbing her bookmark to keep her page, before holding it over his head higher than she could reach. "Finding out the next chapter of this story is more important than finding your mother?"

"Yes…no…it's not that simple." She held her palms up. "Give it back."

"What's wrong?"

"Besides the fact that my husband is holding my manga hostage?"

"Do you know how wrong that sounds?"

"I don't care. Give it back."

"Tell me what's wrong first."

"Why would you think anything is wrong?"

He sent her a long look.

She briefly closed her eyes and rubbed her forehead. "I'm still adjusting. First marrying you by accident—"

"It wasn't an accident."

She ignored his tone and continued, "And then finding out Jackson had secretly married Toyin in Vegas and your mother's passing and my dad's betrayal and lies and…"

"We can at least start searching."

She hugged herself and said in a small voice, "I'm not ready yet."

James hesitated. It wasn't like Ava to be like this. To look so lost and vulnerable. He wanted to comfort her, but he also wanted some answers. "When will you be ready?"

She lowered her head as if ashamed. "I don't know."

"What are you afraid of?"

"I don't want to talk about it."

He gently lifted her chin so she would look at him. "Ava." His voice was a whisper.

"I don't want to face what my father did."

"You've already done that and more. You confronted him. You broke off ties. You're living your life without him and his lies."

"But what if..." She stopped.

"What if what?"

"What if it's too late. What if she has a new family and doesn't want to see me?"

"Edgar said she was looking for you."

"That was before. He said he lost contact years ago. She's gone on with her life. I'd be a shock, a painful reminder of what my father did."

"And seeing you again may be the greatest gift she's ever received. We won't know anything until we try. You're a scientist, you know you can't live on hypothesis."

"I know."

He handed her the manga. "And I know you want this."

"I do." She took the manga and held it close to her chest. "Just not yet." She turned and left the room.

CHAPTER 5

"Clearly she's delusional," Laurence said when Desiree told him the story. They sat together in his cramped apartment finishing off a pot of Dominican tripe stew a paternal aunt had made him and he'd kept frozen.

She set her cracked bowl on the table. Her brother could afford a bigger place and better dishes but he was focused on his FIRE plan, which stood for Financial Independence and Early Retirement. He wasn't too focused on the early retirement aspect since he liked what he did, but the thought of financial independence really motivated him. So he lived considerably below his salary, didn't splurge on many products and budgeted every nickel. He loved to boast that he was on track to total independence by thirty-five. She was happy for him. He had a goal and a dream and he usually succeeded. Although she did wish he would present himself a little better, second hand clothes were all well and good but they should never look that way. She glanced at the frayed cuff of his shirt, determined to find a way to make the item disappear. He was an attractive guy, although not always aware of it and so focused on his plan, he hadn't had many relationships. But he was a good person to talk to.

"I thought so too," Desiree said with a sigh, "but everything else about her is fine and she's scheduled to be released tomorrow. I mean why would she keep it a secret that she had a husband and a child? Do you think Dad knew?"

Laurence shook his head as he stared at his laptop, one of his few splurge items that looked almost as shiny and impressive as when he'd first bought it. "It's hard to know what Dad thinks."

Her brother was right. To cover for their mother's moods their father always appeared upbeat, with a smile, he rarely showed how he felt about something. "True, but to think—"

Laurence shook his head. "Don't get me wrong. I believe her about the crazy ex-husband and secret daughter bit."

"You do?"

"Yes. But what has me worried is *who* she thinks her daughter is. That's insane. There is no way she could be related to Ava Fortune."

"Why not? Who is she?"

Laurence turned the laptop screen to her. Desiree saw a picture of an attractive dark-skinned woman in a white lab coat. "She's a model?"

"No, that lab coat is for real. She's brilliant."

"She's gorgeous."

"And rich and married to a powerful man and...did I mention brilliant? Her background is amazing. She owned a small company that's involved with injectable implants and the science behind her idea of—"

Desiree held up her hand in no mood to hear her brother gush. When he was passionate about something he could talk non-stop for hours. "You're right. There is no way Mom is connected to this woman."

Laurence rubbed his chin suddenly thoughtful. "On the other hand...I mean if we were related, I'd love a chance to meet her and find out how she came up with the idea—"

Desiree closed the laptop. "You're actually salivating."

"You have no idea what this woman has done. Just two minutes of her time would be incredible."

"We're not related. It's not possible. Even if we were," Desiree said when her brother opened his mouth to argue. "What would she think of us? What proof do we have? She'd think we were out to get her money or something."

"We'd tell her the story about Mom and—"

"That won't be enough."

"We can hire someone and then, if we're related, let Mom meet her."

"You'd pay for that?" she said surprised. "You buy toothpaste in bulk to save money."

"For Mom, I'd make an exception."

Desiree sighed. "That sounds reasonable. Let me talk to Mom and see what she says."

But her mother adamantly hated the idea. "No," she said at dinner the next day. Desiree had waited for dinner time, hoping her mother would be more persuaded after eating her favorite red beans and rice (using the Jamaican variation which included coconut milk and garlic as opposed to the Louisiana Creole recipe their father favored). Before dinner she'd asked her father if he'd known about his wife's past and he'd quietly said, "We all have our secrets," before he put spicy zucchini on the table. A statement that wasn't helpful at all. What also wasn't helpful was how silent he was as her mother grew more adamant against Desiree and Laurence's idea. "What if Walter fed her lies about me?"

"I'm sure—"

"You don't know him. You don't know the kind of man he is. If he's still in her life, there's no way I can get close. You have to make sure it's safe. You have to see her first. Find out what she's like, how much she knows, what she thinks of me then I'll know what to do."

"But Mom—"

"There's so much I don't know about her. What are her favorite foods now, what does she like to do?"

"Laurence is looking at her social media profiles."

"That's not enough. I need to know specifics things she wouldn't reveal to the public. The real her."

"You don't have to see her in person at first. We could set up a way for you to do a video conference and meet each other online."

"It wouldn't be the same. I want to touch her cheek,

tell her how much I've always loved her." She took Desiree's hands. "Please do this for me." Desiree looked at her father and he nodded as if saying: Do this for me too. For all of us.

She'd been answering that silent look and request for years.

CHAPTER 6

"You're the only one who has the time." Laurence poured his freshly squeezed orange juice into a thermos as they both stood in his kitchen. One so small she had to plaster herself against the refrigerator door in order not to bump into him. "It's up to you."

Desiree flashed a sour grin. "You don't have to keep reminding me that I'm unemployed."

He gestured to his suit. "The fact that I look like this and am off to work in fifteen minutes and you're," he gestured to her jeans and shirt, "like that with no schedule planned makes it clear."

"And to think I brought you fresh bagels."

"I appreciate it and I have to go." He kissed her on the cheek and left the kitchen. "Great, that's settled."

"It's not settled. How am I supposed to get close to her? How can I find out if Mom's story is true?"

He opened the front door before he turned to her. "You used to work for a private investigator, remember?"

"I kept the office clean. It's not like I really did anything."

"You must have picked up something. And you like to take photographs."

"As a hobby."

"You can figure this out. Mom needs this. And if she is our sister, then she belongs with us." He pointed at her as a parent would a child being left alone for the first time. "Remember to lock up when you leave." He closed the door.

Desiree fell onto the couch. He was right. She was the best person to find out more. But part of her had come over early with his favorite bagels to get him to find another option. Why did it have to be her? Sure, she was the one without a job (not her fault) and Mom had asked her directly (also not her fault she'd just gotten to the hospital before Laurence) but it wasn't fair. Argh!

A sister.

Another life. Her mother had kept secrets all these years. But somehow Desiree wasn't surprised. She'd never felt her mother was fully present. And twice she'd heard her mention the name Amelia. Once when her mother was half asleep, waking from a nap on the couch and another time when she'd looked at a picture of Desiree's high school graduation and said "I wonder what Amelia looks like now?" But when she'd asked her mother who Amelia was she had brushed her question aside.

She always felt she'd had to fight for her mother's

attention and now she knew why. Her mother had a secret pain. A lost child. A child who had left a hole in her heart. A hole that Desiree and her brother had failed to fill. But now she could. Her mother could be whole.

She opened her brother's laptop, which he'd left on the couch, and looked at all the pages filled with Ava's name and beautiful face. If this woman was really her mother's lost daughter she was happy, but part of her was also jealous. Jealous that this woman, who already had so much, would take even more. Her mother would adore her. She would replace Desiree in her mother's heart. The space was already so small it wouldn't be hard to do so.

As much as she wanted to see her mother happy, Ava Hughes Fortune was not someone Desiree could ever compete with. She'd always fallen short in her mother's eyes and this would send her even further. She hoped that her mother was mistaken. That her missing daughter was someone—anyone!—else.

But this reunion would also give her peace as well as pain. All her life all she'd ever wanted, all she'd ever tried to do, was to make her mother happy. Truly, joyously happy. It was her grandest wish.

A wish that never came true.

She remembered when she was about six years old she'd drawn a picture of the family holding hands under a bright yellow sun. She'd hoped her mother would put it up on the fridge so she could see it every day and smile, but she never did. Desiree later found the picture lying soggy and wet in the backyard. Somehow it had survived a Michigan winter.

"Never mind," her father had told her when he'd spotted her holding up the tattered picture. "It probably dropped out of your mother's handbag."

She knew that was a lie. Her father lied to her all the time, she didn't hate him for it, but it didn't make her feel any better either. She knew her mother had likely left the window open and the picture had flown out, it had happened before with Dad's papers, when she'd forgotten about them. And she'd forgotten about her.

Desiree didn't want her mother to not know how much she loved her, how much she wanted her to love her back. She made sure to listen to her, give her gifts, tell her how pretty she was. She would receive small grins, sometimes a chuckle, for her efforts, but they were always so fleeting. But she never stopped trying.

She tried to make others happy too, but that hadn't gone well either. Her first job out of community college was at a private investigator's office. The staff liked her, the owner's daughter didn't. "I hope you don't think you'll last here. The place is going to belong to me so you can tone down the butt kissing."

She left and found another job at a retail store until the other workers said she was making them look bad. The customers loved her, the managers loved her, her colleagues hated her. One had run over her grilled turkey and cheese sandwich with his truck, mashing it before placing it in the staff fridge. She'd found out who it was when she'd overheard him in the hallway bragging to his girlfriend on his cell phone.

She'd lost her job as a house sitter in a swanky neighborhood when one of the clients didn't like how her son looked at her and spread rumors that the recent burglaries were connected to her (they weren't, it was actually her son, but the woman was convinced that Desiree had somehow lured him into a life of crime instead of his actions being the result of her overbearing ways). It was no different when she became a receptionist at a doctor's office. The patients and most of the staff felt that she ran the office well. However, the doctor's husband didn't like her.

"You can keep trying all you want, but just so you know, my wife may like to swing both ways every once in awhile but she doesn't go for fat chicks." He'd whispered one day.

Desiree didn't know how to tell him that first, that was way too much information, second, she wasn't after his wife, and third, she wasn't after anyone's wife or husband or job or promotion. She just wanted to be liked. She wanted others to feel good. She just wanted to do something that she loved to do—make others happy.

She wouldn't call herself a people pleaser. She wouldn't bend over backwards and she didn't see herself as a doormat, but if she could help she'd be the first one at someone's side.

She thought it would be a good thing. But she'd learned it wasn't. Even her relationships fell flat. "It's because you're attracted to melancholy guys who are pathetic," Laurence had once told her. She didn't believe him.

Was it so wrong to fall for a guy who holed himself up in his apartment for weeks on end with the curtains drawn? Didn't he deserve love and someone to bring light into his life? And the biologist who'd just come out of a bad relationship needed someone to listen to him. Really listen. And listen for hours.

But she hadn't been able to make them happy either. So personal relationships were off the table for now. Instead, she'd focus on one goal: Making her mother happy. This was her chance.

But this time it felt like a burden, failing this would send her mother into a deep depression, so she did what she always did when she felt trapped. She got in her car, drove to a park, and blared a little death metal and hard rock music and sang at the top of her lungs until her throat ached and then she pulled out her cell phone and wrote him.

Him. Million. The man who had kept her sane for the past five years. After leaving Felice's room, she felt oddly comforted by writing to Felice's brother and had kept it up in her journal. It made her feel less alone. Her fantasy Million patiently read every letter and understood how she felt. She'd filled more than a dozen journals (both written and electronic) with letters to him. She'd given him more traits. She knew how tall he was, what kind of car he drove, what kind of clothes he wore. How he liked to spend his time. He'd been a true confidant and secret lover. Although, in truth, she never fantasized about him in that way. Just as a soul mate. Someone she could turn to. Today wouldn't be any different.

Dear M,

You wouldn't believe this. I might have a half sister. Not just anyone, but some gorgeous genius that mom will probably instantly fall in love with, in a way that she's never loved me. Do you know what that feels like? To want someone to love you so bad it hurts? You probably do but won't admit it so that will be our secret. I hope your father is leaving you alone. I wish I could see Felice again.

I'm scared. Your sister said you aren't scared of anything and I wish I could say the same. I'm scared I'm going to screw this up.

Wish me luck. I'll write again soon.

A friend

" ook at that. Some dumbass retard is in the middle of the road."

Desiree opened her mouth outraged by her driver's offensive words and tone; she'd liked the talkative woman, with big earrings in the shape of strawberries, who had pictures of her grandkids on the visor, until this moment. She'd decided to hire a driver instead of using her own car (the nearly hour drive would cost her, but she'd get the money back from Laurence) so that she could get close to the Fortunes without any identifying features (like her distinctive purple Acura that she'd inherited from a friend who'd decided to hike across Europe). In recent articles, Desiree had discovered that Ava Fortune had mentioned the shop of her brother-in-law, Rudy, where he designed and created art pieces.

Desiree made a plan to go visit the shop and see what she could learn about the Fortunes. Kirkland, Virginia was settled in a wealthy county known for its high end shops and leafy green suburbs. She was instantly impressed by the picture perfect main street, where the shop was located, and liked the feel of the town, even though she knew the prices were hardly for the ordinary person. She was only a few blocks away from her destination when the driver's words shocked her.

Then she saw what the driver was talking about and the angry scold she was about to give died on her lips.

A young black man with Down's Syndrome stood in the center of the crosswalk with his eyes closed, waving his hands, between covering his ears, clearly in distress while cars zipped past him. "Pull over here."

"You're not going to help this—"

"How much do I owe you?"

The woman told her the amount and Desiree paid the fare then jumped out of the car. She knew once the light changed the man may be too traumatized to move and she needed to help him. Just as she made it to the crosswalk, the traffic light changed, the cars stopped, but the man didn't move. She dashed over to him and lightly touched his arm. "You're okay now," she said keeping her voice soft, but bright, in order not to startle him. "Let's cross here. Come on."

She was halfway to the other side of the road when a large black man in a dark suit appeared in front of them. He looked furious. Desiree wondered if he was one of the driver's who wanted to confront the younger man. Her protective instincts kicked into gear even though the other man secretly terrified her, although he looked sort of familiar and she didn't know why.

"He didn't mean it," she said in the other man's

defense. "I'm sure he got a little turned around but he's fine now. And no one was hurt."

It took her only a few seconds to realize that the man wasn't looking at her. His gaze hadn't left the younger man's face. She didn't want him to get into trouble. "Honey, where were you trying to go?"

"How many times have I told you not to run across the street like that?" the other man interrupted her, his voice a low growl.

The younger man lowered his head. "She saw me and she didn't say hi. I wanted her to say hi."

"I don't care."

His lower lip trembled. "You're angry."

The bigger man rested his hands on his hips. "I'm very angry."

The younger man gripped his hand into a fist. He kept his head lowered but his voice filled with anger and pain. "I'm mad too. Very mad. Why didn't she say hi? I liked her. I really liked her. And she doesn't like me anymore. It hurts so bad."

To Desiree's shock she watched the older man gently rub his knuckles against the younger man's cheek. He said, "I know," before pulling him close and hugging him.

"Why does it hurt?" the other man cried.

"Love does that."

"Ice cream helps," Desiree said brightly. The fierce looking man finally turned his dark gaze to her and she felt heat stealing into her cheeks. She probably should have kept her mouth shut. They obviously knew each other and clearly this man didn't want her to be there. But for some reason she wanted him to like her and know that she'd only wanted to help. However, his look told her she'd failed. She took a step back.

"Your treat?" the man said.

She blinked surprised by the question and the slight smile on his lips. "Uh sure."

inutes later they sat in an airy ice cream shop surrounded by pink and green pastel colors splashed on the walls in a playful display with three sundaes in glass containers sitting on a bright pink table.

"My name is James," the fierce looking man said by way of introduction, "and this is my younger brother, Rudy."

Desiree shook his hand. He looked like a James and he looked like someone else too. But who? "Desiree, nice to meet you."

Rudy folded his arms. "I'm not hungry."

James picked up his spoon unconcerned. "Just eat a few bites."

Desiree lifted the sleeve of her white blouse and held her arm out to him. "See this scar? It hurt a lot when I first got it as a kid. I cried and cried. But over time it healed. You can touch it if you want."

Rudy looked at the scar in awe then lightly ran his forefinger over it.

"It's the same on the inside," Desiree continued. "You cry because it hurts, but one day you'll be better. It won't go away, but it won't hurt anymore. Okay?"

Rudy looked at her for a long moment before he nodded then dipped into his sundae. "I don't know why she doesn't like me anymore."

"You're right. But it's better to be with people who like you than people who don't. And I like you very much and I just met you."

James playfully nudged him. "Go Rudy, you know we have a way with the ladies. Especially pretty ones."

A shadow of a smile touched his lips and he ate his ice cream with more interest. And to her surprise, Desiree felt heat steal into her cheeks once again. Who was with this guy and why was he making her blush?

"How did you get that scar?" James asked.

"Jumping out of a burning building."

James held up his hands. "Sorry I asked."

"No, it's true."

He stared at her shocked. "You were in a burning building?"

She nodded. "My mother...she started a gas fire in the kitchen at one of our apartments. I was racing to get my brother and dog and tripped and cut my arm on something sharp. I still don't know what it was."

"Did they make it?" Rudy asked with wide eyes.

Desiree frowned. "Make it?"

"The dog and your brother?"

"Yes, thankfully we all got out in time. It was really scary."

"How old were you?" James asked.

"Seven."

"Brave kid."

She shrugged, embarrassed by the admiration in his voice. "You do what you have to in order to survive."

"What do you do for a living?"

She hesitated. What was with the questions? And his piercing gaze was a little unnerving. She'd noticed the gold band on his finger so he was married and not interested in her in that way. What would he do if he found out she was unemployed? "Oh...I do odd jobs here and there."

"Anything in particular right now?"

"Do you have a job offer?"

To her relief he lowered his gaze and his voice. "I might."

Really? Was this guy serious? He certainly looked like someone who didn't joke often. "And I might be interested, but that depends on what the job is."

He nodded, pensive. "Fair enough. I—" His cell phone beeped. He looked down at the screen, softly swore then said, "I've got to go. Are you free tomorrow? I'd like to talk to you. We can meet here again say...three?"

"Fine."

"Come on Rudy."

"I haven't finished my sundae yet."

"You can finish it later."

"But I don't—"

"You can take it with you," Desiree said quickly, wanting to sidestep an argument. "That's why I got it in this container," she said putting a cover over the clear glass bowl. It had cost a little extra (plus she wasn't used to paying for ice cream that cost nearly as much as cell phone bill and wanted a souvenir) but it had been worth it. "And you can use it again at home. You can come up with your own mixture. It's a special bowl." She handed the dish to him.

"But it will melt."

"We'll be home in no time," James said.

"And the bowl will keep it cold for a good while longer," Desiree said.

Rudy nodded, satisfied. "Okay."

James looked at her relieved. He handed her his card. "Thanks for the ice cream."

"No problem."

Desiree watched the two men leave surprised by how empty and lonely her table felt without them. She'd eaten by herself before but their sudden departure made her aware of how often that had become lately.

She sighed wistful. James was a beautiful man. But married. What a bummer, it was easier to fantasize about a guy when you knew they were single. Not that she'd even consider a man like him, or that he'd consider her. His shoes alone cost several rent payments. But whoever was married to him was a lucky woman. What was his surname again? She didn't remember him telling her. She looked down at the business card. "James Fortune, BioMed Solutions." Her heart stopped. Wait. James Fortune? *The* James *Fortune?*

She jumped to her feet with such force she knocked her chair over, startling the couple at the next table. She quickly set it right, her heart pounding. That man was James Fortune? The one married to Ava Hughes Fortune, her half-sister? Possible half-sister? Really?

And his brother Rudy? That's why he looked so familiar. In pictures he was striking but in real life he was even more impressive. How had her sister managed to land a man like him? But of course what man wouldn't want a gorgeous, successful woman by his side? Ava probably hadn't had to work hard to catch his interest. Women like her rarely did.

Somehow, what had truly surprised her about him, aside from how intimidating he looked, was he was more approachable than she'd expected them to be. While he didn't smile when placing his order, he didn't have the condescending air she would have expected from someone with his status.

Although intimidating in person, he was kind too. The way he had been with his brother was amazing. And he wanted to offer her a job? This was better than expected. If she could get close to the family this way she could find out more. She didn't want to spring her mother's strange story on them. It shouldn't take more than a week for her to verify a few things then she'd reveal herself. If all went well, she'd have her mother smiling by next Saturday.

CHAPTER 9

His brother's grins usually made him nervous.

When James walked through the front door, stood in the foyer, and his identical twin brother, Jackson, greeted him and Rudy with a grin, James's heart fell.

"Edgar's mad, isn't he?"

Jackson's grin widened and dressed in a orange suit with dark trim he reminded James of a smug tiger. "Only if you believe in understatement."

That meant his stepfather was chewing nails. James silently swore.

"I'm putting my ice cream away," Rudy said, cradling his sundae like a rugby player facing his opponents. He hurried to the kitchen.

James closed the door behind him. "Is he in the study or on the balcony?"

Jackson's lip twitched, his brother was enjoying this a little too much. "He's in the kitchen."

James softly swore again. That meant he couldn't avoid him and he couldn't let Rudy explain why they'd been delayed.

"It's not like you to be late. You were supposed to pick Rudy up and then come here for a conference call with a South African contact. What happened?"

James headed down the hall towards the kitchen. "Something came up."

"What?"

"We met a nice lady," they both heard Rudy tell Edgar in the large kitchen, his voice seeming to echo off the three steel refrigerators and black granite countertops.

James looked at his stepfather who stood by the counter with a glass of papaya juice. He didn't look angry, but James knew he was. "It wasn't like that."

"And she bought us ice cream," Rudy continued delighted.

James shook his head. "It wasn't like that either."

"And she let me touch her—"

"That's enough, Rudy," James said. "Do you want to tell them *why* she did those things?"

Rudy fell silent.

"What happened?" Jackson asked.

"I'll tell you later." James patted his brother on the back. "Is your ice cream in the freezer now?"

He nodded.

"Okay then. Go on."

Rudy sent him a cautious look.

"No, I'm not angry anymore."

Rudy looked relieved before he left.

The two men pinned James with a stare—one amused, the other demanding. "What happened?" they both said.

James pulled out a chair from under the kitchen table and sat. "When we were walking to the car, Rudy saw Lucy from across the street and shouted out 'hello'. It was obvious she was ignoring him, but he didn't understand that so he...he ran into the road to get to her and then the traffic light changed just as he was halfway across."

"You let that happen?" Edgar said anger in his voice.

"It happened so fast I didn't even know he wasn't behind me until I turned around. I heard him call out to her, but didn't think...Look, I know I should have been more careful. If it's any help, I lost a decade off my life and aged in an instant."

Jackson shook his head. "No, it's your clothes that have that effect."

James ignored him and looked at Edgar. "It won't happen again. I apologize."

Edgar nodded then left.

Once he was out of hearing, James pointed at his brother. "This is your fault."

His brows shot up. "Your poor taste in clothes is my fault?"

James threw up his hands exasperated. "I'm not talking about clothes, I'm talking about Rudy. You said, 'Let him have a girlfriend. What could be the harm?' I can't believe we listened to you."

Jackson scratched his cheek, thoughtful. "I didn't say it would be perfect. He's a man."

"He's not a—"

Jackson sat down in front of him. "He's still a man. And he has needs like the rest of us. Relax, I taught him how to use a condom."

"You did what?"

"It's a precaution. He's a Fortune all we need is some woman claiming that he...you know. Put a bun in the oven. Popped a penny in the jar. Planted his seed in—"

"You think this is funny?"

"No, I'm just letting you know he's very responsible."

"Well now he's devastated."

"Well she's a bitch."

"She's not a bitch." Lucy was a sweet girl, who always wore a plastic daisy in her hair, Rudy had met at the recreation center that organized trips, conducted skills courses and socialization for people with cognitive differences. She had a job packing bags at the local grocery store. And while he would have preferred she'd handled the breakup better, he didn't like Jackson's harsh assessment of her.

"Yes, she is. She could have said 'hi'. They could have been friends."

"I think that a relationship like this is too much for him."

"He'll get over it," Jackson said with little concern. "I'll talk to him."

"I don't think you need to have any more 'special talks' with him. You'll be telling him about strip clubs next."

"No, already did that. Took him to one and we hardly got through the front door."

"When was that?"

"A couple years ago."

James pinched the bridge of his nose. "Was it the night he came back and had nightmares?" He glared at his brother. "You told me you'd taken him to a scary movie."

"That's what I told him. For some reason the whips and chains really freaked him out. But the women were—"

"Jackson—"

"I was trying to expose him."

"He doesn't need that kind of exposure."

Jackson fell quiet for a long moment then said, "Has he told you he wants to get married?"

"Well, sure but..."

"You didn't believe him or you didn't take him seriously? Which one is it?"

James sighed, conflicted. He wanted to protect his brother, but also understood his needs. He swore.

Jackson nodded. "Exactly. He told me he wants a wedding like you and Ava. He wants to hold hands and kiss and...that's about as far as he goes. We're lucky, he's not as sexually driven as others, but the time could come."

"I met somebody."

"So you're ready to tell Ava you've met someone else?"

James shot him a look. Even though Jackson's relationship with Ava wasn't as contentious as it had been in the past, he still didn't like his brother's casual jabs about her, especially when he was still worried about Rudy.

Jackson cleared his throat, sensing the change in his

brother's mood and straightened in his seat. "Okay, I'm ready to be serious."

"I'm thinking of hiring someone to shadow him for a while."

"Who...wait. Not the ice cream lady?"

James nodded.

"The one you just met?"

"He liked her and there was something about her that felt...right. Almost familiar. She reminded me of someone. Don't worry. I'll look into her background."

"Is she pretty?"

James frowned. "I thought you were ready to be serious."

"I am being serious."

"You'll find out when you meet her. I haven't gotten a chance to talk to her yet, but I thought you should know."

Jackson sighed. "Fine."

He knew there was nothing more his brother could say. Rudy wanted to take courses at the local college and his recent helper had quit due to a family emergency and another individual they'd hired hadn't been a good fit. With the breakup of Lucy he didn't want to expose him to too much change.

"Do you think she'll say yes?"

"I hope so."

"I can be more persuasive."

"But I saw her first."

CHAPTER 10

*D*esiree stared at James in shock.

It wasn't the look she'd hoped to have. She'd spent extra care this morning getting ready for their meeting, but now she imagined staring at him like a fish. Had she heard right? "You want me to be his companion?"

"He's taking courses at the community college. We had someone but she left and I don't have time in my schedule. It will only be for about eight weeks. You can stay with us or we'll have a car pick you up. It will be about eight hours a week. He still wants to focus on his business while doing this. With him you'll go over the course notes, he likes to be challenged, but not pressured. There are certain adjustments you'll need to make to help him achieve his goal, but you seemed to have a way with him."

"Did his other companion stay with you?"

"Yes, but she was trained to work with people with my brother's needs."

"I see."

"He's very smart, if you saw his jewelry designs and store you'd be amazed at—"

"You don't have to sell him to me."

"I know that not everyone feels comfortable around a guy like Rudy."

"It's not that. It's..." She didn't even know why she was hesitating. How could she say no? This was almost too good to be true. She could stay at their place? Get close to Ava and find out what she needed to know? But she hated lying. However, it was for a good cause. Eight weeks and then she'd tell them the truth. Her mother would understand and she needed the work. The salary he'd quoted would last a long time and she could use time away from her boring apartment.

She held out her hand and smiled. "It sounds perfect."

THAT EVENING Laurence looked at his sister unsure he'd heard her correctly. They sat in his living room with a Chinese takeaway he'd reheated. "You got a job with the Fortunes?"

Desiree bit into a rubbery pot sticker. "Yes, I'll be working with their youngest brother for the next eight weeks."

"Did you talk to Mom yet?"

"No, I thought you could talk to her for me." She ate

some rice then set her chopsticks down, the rice tasted old and felt hard. She didn't dare ask how long he'd kept this meal in the freezer.

"Why?"

"Because she won't want me to do this and I could really use the money, plus Rudy has gone through a lot and I would hate to work with him and then leave after a week. Tell her that this is the best way I can find out all I can about Ava's habits so that when they finally meet she won't feel like a stranger."

He shook his head unsure. "I don't know, it sounds like a risk."

"They're already doing a background check, there's nothing that will connect us. Mom lives under her new married name and I've got some solid references. I'll do a good job. I'm not really lying to them."

"Except the fact that you're scoping them out like a spy."

Desiree frowned. "Don't say it like that. I feel guilty enough. Mom wanted me to find out if her ex-husband is still in the picture, this will be a great way to know if that's true. Plus, I really like James."

"Oooh, Jamesss, you're already on a first name basis. Does my sister have a crush?"

"Shut up."

"I can't believe you think it's okay to work for your possible half-sister's husband."

"I thought you wanted to know how she came up with her injectable limb."

His voice turned eager. "You'd ask her for me?"

"Of course. I'll even tell her a little about you so when you finally meet she'll be impressed."

"Well, I guess I can convince Mom to wait a little longer."

Desiree grinned knowing he was hooked. "Thank you."

CHAPTER 11

He'd been holding his breath.

James hadn't realized that until he'd gotten Desiree's report back. The fact that her background check came up clean relieved him more than he'd expected. Somehow he'd wanted it to be so. He didn't know why, but he felt as if she was someone his family needed. But he was also nervous. He didn't like when things felt too perfect. Too convenient.

But there was something about the situation that felt almost too right. That she'd be there for Rudy, that she was unemployed just when they needed someone. He'd grown cynical and wary of coincidences, but also there was something about her that bothered him. He couldn't figure out why.

He wasn't used to someone so bright and bubbly. He'd been impressed to discover she'd worked in a hospital as a patient service representative. She had such an easy wide grin. He liked her. He didn't usually like people quickly, but she was different. He hoped Ava and Edgar liked her too.

"I've hired someone to shadow Rudy. They'll be staying with us," he told them both at dinner after Rudy had excused himself. The meal had boasted a clear display of the brothers' Grenadian background with a starter of callaloo soup and a one pot mixture of salted chicken, breadfruit, dumplings, sweet potatoes and a host of other vegetables.

"Fine," Edgar said, pushing himself from the table. "As long as she stays out of my way." He left.

Ava set her fork down and clasped her hands together. "Is that really necessary? I could adjust my schedule."

"I think he needs someone besides us to talk to about his breakup with Lucy and I think she'll keep him distracted."

"Is she from one of the agencies?"

He hesitated. This was going to be the tricky part. "She's a freelancer."

"How did you get her references?"

"I didn't need one. I met her and liked her. She's done many different things." Too many if he was honest, but Ava didn't need to know that.

"Where did you meet her?"

"Why all the questions?"

"Why the hesitation?"

He sighed. "She saved Rudy the other day. She calmed him down, made him smile and...and I offered her a job."

"And you think it's a good idea to invite a random

stranger into our house because she made Rudy smile? You know he's your biggest weak spot."

He sent her a knowing look. "No, not my biggest."

Ava couldn't stop a smile. "Okay, you're *second* biggest after me. You trust her?"

"She saved her brother and dog from a fire."

Ava started to laugh. "Are you serious?"

"That's what she told me," James said sounding a little hurt.

"And you believed her?"

"Yes, plus I verified it. Aside from the scar I saw I followed up on the story. The medical records checked out."

Ava blinked. "You shouldn't have access to them."

He nodded. "That's right, so you can pretend I didn't tell you that. I want you to know I dug deep to make sure I'm not putting our family at risk. I think you'll like her."

Ava narrowed her eyes. "You seem to like her enough for both of us."

CHAPTER 12

*A*va Fortune really had it all. Gorgeous house, gorgeous husband, gorgeous figure. If she hadn't found her so beautiful and terrifying, Desiree would have hated her.

Instead she sat in the kitchen nook facing her, afraid of touching the ice tea the housekeeper had placed on the table, terrified she would drop it. She'd told James that she didn't want a fuss, but he'd had someone take her bags to her room and ushered her into the kitchen to meet his wife.

But instead of feeling greeted, she felt like she was meeting a royal figure who had the power to get her head chopped off. She didn't know what her mother's first husband looked like, but she could see her brother's coloring in Ava and the certain way their nose and eyes came together was a key trait from their mother. However any other similarities ended there.

Desiree cleared her throat. "It's a p-pleasure to me-meet you, Mrs. Fortune."

Ava grinned. "You don't have to be so formal or nervous. Call me Ava."

"Desiree."

"I know."

Desiree inwardly cringed. Of course she'd know that. "I just...want to do a good job."

"If James trusts you, you've already succeeded. Do you have any questions for us?"

More than you know. "James...I mean Mr. Fortune...uh your husband sent me the details of his—uh Rudy's schedule."

James placed a friendly hand on her shoulder. "What's got you so jumpy all of a sudden? Do you need some ice cream to calm you down?"

"No, I'm sorry." She rubbed her hands on her jeans. If she didn't calm down she could lose this opportunity. "I've never been this lucky before. I really need this job." At least that was the truth.

Ava nodded. "I see."

But Desiree didn't know what that meant. She couldn't read the other woman's expression. She doubted she'd ever worried about keeping a job in her life. Women like her didn't have jobs. They had careers. Professions. They didn't need CVs they had *reputations*.

Ava pushed her chair back. "I have to dash, but I hope you'll feel at home." She turned to James. "I'm going to the lab."

"Okay."

Desiree watched her go then sank back in her chair,

her heart racing. It took her a moment to realize James was watching her.

"What happened?" he asked her.

"I'm sorry. She's so amazing. I didn't know how to get a hold of myself."

"She's also taken." He pointed to his ring.

Desiree widened her eyes. "Oh, no it's not like that." A soft smile touched his lips and she wasn't sure if he was teasing her or not but she didn't want any misunderstanding between them. "I'm not attracted to her. And even if I were I wouldn't..." She shook her head. "Never mind. She's...you're a lucky man, she's so smart and beautiful."

"Don't be fooled," another voice said from the doorway. She turned and saw a man wearing a bright red blazer, gold neckerchief and dark trousers. A man who looked exactly like James. If James liked flashy clothes and sported a sexy grin. The other man approached the table. "When the clock strikes—"

"Ignore him," James said.

The other man held out his hand. "As if that's even possible," he said with a sniff. "Jackson."

"Desiree."

"What are you doing here?" James asked him annoyed. "Don't you have someone at home to play with? Oh, that's right. Toyin's away at a retail conference." James pulled a face and said in a mocking tone, "Are you lonely?"

Jackson ignored his brother's teasing and let his dark gaze survey Desiree in playful intrigue. "Since you wouldn't describe her, I had to see for myself."

He was a flirt. She could deal with a flirt. Desiree batted her eyelashes at him and cupped her face in her hands. "Do I pass?"

Instead of making him smile, he frowned and took the chair that Ava had vacated. He looked at James. "You're right. She does seem familiar." He turned to her. "Have we met before?"

Her heart started to pound. It was bad enough to have two identically gorgeous guys staring at her, even worse to have them suspicious. But why would they be suspicious? She looked nothing like Ava. "It's possible," she said in a bright voice. She had to charm them, make them like her. That's what she was good at. "I've done a lot of odd jobs in the past."

He nodded. "Don't let Ava scare you. But if she does or if you have any questions, feel free to call—"

"Me," James said.

Jackson shot him a look, as if annoyed that his brother was ruining his fun. James blinked, bored. Jackson shrugged. "And if you can't get a straight answer from him, call me."

"But first, lie down and take two aspirin and wait for the feeling to go away."

Jackson flashed a sour grin and playfully hit his brother on the arm. "Such a kidder. Nice to meet you." He stood and walked away.

James shook his head. "I'm not kidding. Come to me first. My brother's smart, but he also likes to get into trouble."

She bit her lip. "Does he like Ava?"

James's gaze sharpened. "Why do you ask?"

"I just...never mind. It's none of my business."

"It's complicated. He likes to tease her because...it's all in good fun. We're a close family."

"Of course."

"Let me just say that they dated for a while, but she ended up preferring me."

"And he's jealous?"

"No," James said then stood, effectively ending any more questions. "I think it's time you see your room."

Ava had dated twin brothers? What a bold woman. And she suspected she could get more out of Jackson than James, but she'd learned that Jackson didn't live there. That would be difficult but eight weeks was enough time to bump into him again and she was certain she could get his number.

That night she wrote to Million.

You will not believe where I am right now. Or this room. It's out of a strange sci-fi fantasy I've never had. It's odd but beautiful at the same time and larger than my apartment. I almost made a fool out of myself when I met Ava. I hope I do better when I see her again, but I really like James. Not that you have to be jealous. He's her husband and seems devoted to her. His twin brother on the other hand might have some information about her that might prove useful. We'll see. Right now I'm going to take a long shower in a bathroom that could double as a spa suite—it has one of those huge waterfall showerheads—and then sleep.

Wish you were here to share it all with me.

Desiree looked at the last sentence and paused surprised by how much the sentence felt true. She did wish he was there. That he was no longer a figment of her imagination. It could be because she felt, for the first time, that she was in a place that suited him. She knew he came from money. She imagined him to be of medium height (she didn't mind tall men as long as they weren't too tall or broad, she found that build too intimidating) beautifully muscular with a sexy grin. This mansion and bedroom (with its high ceilings and large windows) would seem normal to him, but she briefly wondered what his bare body would look like as he stood under the rushing water in the shower, how the sheets would sound against his skin as he lay in bed beside her. What the touch of his hand would feel like against her cheek, the feel of his lips...

Desiree closed her eyes and shook her head. Where had that thought come from? While her writings to him hadn't always been G-rated, she'd never thought of him like this before. She thought of him as a friend and confidant (sometimes PG-rated lover) nothing more. She was just anxious and lonely and this incredible room had her thinking strange thoughts. She had to focus on her two missions, keeping Rudy happy and uncovering as much about Ava Fortune as she could.

CHAPTER 13

It probably wasn't normal to gasp at the sight of one's husband at the breakfast table, but Toyin did just that when she returned home from the airport and saw Jackson sitting there half asleep. He cupped his chin in his hand and had his eyes closed. But even unshaven he looked like a clothing ad for morning wear. He was dressed in a maroon silk robe.

Jackson was not a morning person. He could barely put coherent words together before ten am. It was just eight-thirty.

She rushed over to him and touched his forehead. "Are you okay? Did something happen?"

"Welcome home."

He didn't smell like alcohol. Actually he smelled really good, like mint. "Jackson, what are you doing up?"

He pulled her onto his lap. "I wanted to see you."

She tried to wiggle off his lap, but he kept his hold.

Even tired he was stronger than her. She relented with a sigh. "You'd see me later."

He rested his forehead against her arm. "Did you eat? I had Bo make you something."

She sighed, wondering how much he'd bothered his poor assistant. "Come on. Let's get you back to bed."

He shook his head, tightening his grip. "I need to tell you something before I do. I don't want to forget it."

"Can't it wait?"

"No. Something's bothering me."

"Okay, what is it?"

"I met her. I met this woman."

Toyin grinned amused. "Should I be jealous?"

"What?"

She bit back a laugh. It was too early to tease him. He wouldn't get the humor. "Never mind. Go on."

"James hired her to be with Rudy during his college courses and help him at home with his studies too."

"That's good."

"I know, it should be but something about her...reminds me of someone."

"Bad?"

"I don't know. I just feel like something's off. And I shouldn't. James is usually better than me when it comes to women."

"Oh, thanks," Toyin said with mock outrage.

Jackson was too tired to notice. "So I shouldn't feel this way, but...I just had to tell someone. It's probably nothing."

"Probably. Now come on."

"Missed you."

"When you wake up I'll show you what I brought back for you." She also wanted to share the information she'd gathered that would help her store, New Worlds, and possibly the costume store owner down the street she'd recently befriended whose business was failing.

"I doubt anything you brought back will be better than what's sitting on my lap right now."

She grinned and kissed him before wrapping her arms around his neck. "You're such a romantic." Then she whispered, "I missed you too."

And he held her close, making her feel warm and safe. It was good to be home.

CHAPTER 14

It took nearly four weeks to realize she was in trouble.

Desiree had done her best to make sure Rudy liked her, that the family liked her. But she'd never tried to make him fall in love with her. He'd been vulnerable. She should have been more cautious and had suspected his feelings for her were deeper than mere friendship. It was one Friday afternoon while they were in one of the study rooms on campus that she had her suspicions confirmed.

"I really like you," Rudy said.

"I like you too."

"And you don't have a boyfriend."

"Nope." It was the fourth time he'd asked her that.

He put an item on the table. It took Desiree one horrified moment to identify it as a ring before Rudy said, "Would you marry me?"

She was scared to move. The ring was beautiful— made of tiny silver loops—so were his innocent brown eyes, but she couldn't say yes. She didn't know what to say.

He pushed the ring closer to her. "I made it for you."

She didn't want to hurt his feelings. She should have been a little more careful. "I can't."

"Why not? You like me and I like you. My brothers got married and I want to get married too. You'll be a pretty bride and my Dad will get me a suit and…"

She stopped listening, her mind racing. How could this have happened? Where had she gone wrong? She'd wanted him to like her but not this much. Had other companions had similar issues? Wouldn't James have told her if they had? She rubbed her hands together under the table. She had to tell him something. How could she tell him why she couldn't marry him without making things worse? She inwardly swore. No wonder he kept asking her if she had a boyfriend. She'd thought it was simple curiosity. She didn't want to get fired. Plus, he'd already had his heart broken recently. She didn't want to be the next one in line. How could she save his pride? "The reason I can't marry you is because I have a secret. Can you keep a secret?"

He nodded.

She took a deep breath. Even though Rudy was easily impressionable it was okay for a little lie that no one else would find out about.

"I'm already getting married."

"You are?"

"Yes. His name is…" She looked at his T-shirt and saw a swirl logo and the name Duchamp printed underneath. Duchamp. That sounded like a good surname and now for a first name... She'd been writing to her fantasy Million for years but that wouldn't cut it as the name of her beloved. Maxwell, Maddox, Maximillian. Yes! That was it. Something she could easily remember. "Maximillian Duchamp," she said.

Rudy looked at her with wide eyes, shocked. "Really?"

His shock was actually a little annoying. She'd expected him to be surprised, intrigued, but he looked stunned. As if she'd said she was going to marry the prince of a grand nation. Why was it so amazing that she'd be engaged to a man with such an impressive name? "And it's a secret. Nobody knows about us. Except you."

"You're gonna marry Maximillian Duchamp?"

"Yes," Desiree said warming to the idea. Ava didn't need to be the only one to have someone incredible interested in her. "Sometimes I call him Million just to annoy him, but I think he secretly likes it. He's very good looking and successful. Just like the Fortune men," she said with a wink, making Rudy smile. "He started two companies before the age of twenty-one and knocked me off my feet. I couldn't help myself. He's a black belt in Brazilian jiu-jitsu. He's an amazing swimmer and I love his little dog AP too."

"Why aren't you wearing a ring?"

"Because it's a secret, remember? His...family doesn't know about me, except for his sister. She travels a lot and she's the one who introduced us and she loves me to bits but anyway, he's afraid his father wouldn't agree so we've kept this under wraps." She lowered her voice. "His father can be very scary."

"So you can't get married?"

"Nope."

"Do you love him?"

"Of course I do and he loves me. Very much." She rested a hand over her heart and said with a tragic sigh, "But we're destined to be apart."

"Forever?"

She nodded. "Forever."

Rudy looked near tears. "That's very sad."

"That's okay," Desiree said, pretending to put on a brave face. She touched his hand. "I'm okay. Don't look like that. But now you understand why I can't marry you. But we'll always be friends."

CHAPTER 15

"I know a secret."

James looked up from his laptop and studied his brother Rudy who had a worried look on his face. He'd walked into the great room, where James worked and Ava sat wearing her favorite Tim Hortons long sleeve T-shirt and reading something on her tablet, with an eagerness he hadn't seen in a while. The last time he'd been this way was when he'd wanted to go on a trip hiking with his friends and had been afraid his family would say no. "Is it a good secret or a bad secret?"

"It's a sad one."

"Is it yours?"

"No."

"Whose is it?"

"Desiree's."

"If it's not your secret then you shouldn't tell us about it," Ava said.

"But—"

"Rudy hates keeping secrets," James said. "And Mom taught him keeping a secret wasn't good. It's kept him safe." He turned to Rudy. "Go on and tell us."

"Desiree's getting married to Maximillian Duchamp."

James blinked.

Ava stared.

"Desiree's getting married to Maximillian Duchamp," Rudy repeated a little louder in case they hadn't heard him the first time.

"That's impossible," James finally said.

"It's true. She told me."

"It must be another Max Duchamp."

"She says he liked Brazilian jetson."

"Jiu-jitsu?" James corrected.

Rudy nodded. "A black belt. And she said that he has a sister who really likes her and a scary dad and a little dog."

Ava stared at James stunned. "I don't believe he'd be engaged and not tell us, do you?"

James scratched his chin. "A man has a right to his secrets."

"And do you really think he'd be engaged to a woman like her?"

James sent her a look. "Like what? It's not like you to be a snob."

"I'm not being a snob."

"She's attractive. She's funny. Caring. A wonderful woman."

Ava frowned. "Which sounds perfect, except we're talking about *Max*, not you."

He nodded. "True."

Rudy took a seat and rubbed his hands together eager to share more. "And Desiree's really sad because she doesn't get to see him. I want to help her."

"I don't think we should get involved," Ava said.

"Please, James," Rudy said. "She really wants to see him."

James sighed seeing the hope in his brother's eyes. "Okay, Rudy, here's what I'm going to do."

CHAPTER 16

A liar.

Max couldn't stand liars. He'd fallen in love and nearly married one and vowed never to be a victim again. He wouldn't be someone's prey.

One thing he knew for certain was that James Fortune wasn't a liar; however, from what his friend had just told him, he was in the presence of one. Max would have to tread carefully to gather as much intel so that he could keep both his friend and his own reputation safe. If the phone call he'd answered in his study had come from anyone besides James Fortune, a man who he could trust, and he trusted few people, he would have thought he was joking when he told him that he'd found out about Max's secret fiancée. He looked at the black and white photograph of a desolate wasteland he had on his wall: A reminder that one is either a conqueror or conquered.

"Fiancée?" he repeated just to make sure he'd heard correctly.

"Yes. She's working with Rudy and told him all about you. In detail. I thought you should know since Rudy isn't one to keep secrets. I don't think she meant to tell him on purpose, but rumors can spread. I thought I should warn you."

He wouldn't let James know how important this warning was until he found out who he was dealing with. What kind of liar had come into their midst? He wouldn't deny anything, not yet. He was glad that James wasn't the kind of guy to ask questions such as why he hadn't told them he was seeing someone or how long had he kept the secret. His friend was too well mannered to pry. He liked him for that. "Thanks."

"Rudy has his heart set on seeing you together. She's a special woman. I'm not surprised you wanted to keep her to yourself."

Max gripped his free hand into a fist. This woman was a charmer. That made her even more dangerous. "Hmm."

"She's staying at my place for awhile. Did she tell you that?"

"No." At least that was true. He didn't like lying to his friend, but he had to be careful. If he told James the truth the woman could disappear without being caught.

"So if you want to see her and talk about what to do next, feel free."

"Thank you. I'd like that." They set up a time before he set down the phone. Why would this woman lie about him? Perhaps she wanted the Fortunes to pay her more money. That seemed like a typical ploy.

He was used to being a target. As the son of a

successful businessman who owned a number of high end clubs along the East, South and Midwest, a lucrative lighting effects company with clients both stateside and abroad plus Max's own various interests, he'd grown used to people using his name, reputation, or trust to get what they wanted. He'd learned to let people underestimate him because he'd been trained by the best. Trained by someone who had ripped out his heart and nearly destroyed his family. It was the first time he'd been a victim, been made a fool of—something his father would never let him forget.

"Didn't seeing your grandfather teach you anything?" his father told him after his broken engagement and the aftermath that followed. "This is what happens when you don't follow my lead."

Flashes of the monster house reentered his memory. He didn't want to end up there alone, a broken old man. He'd remembered what his grandfather had whispered to him, the strange, but oddly chilling words, but as his father had predicted listening to anything his grandfather said came with a price. He'd tried to defy his father. It had worked in the past. While he never became a stellar student or showed much interest in his father's two businesses he liked the idea of being an entrepreneur (creating two small business while still in high school) and after a growth spurt at seventeen that led to a skinny, gangly body that made him clumsy, he took up Brazilian jiu-jitsu ultimately earning a black belt. The control of the art form had so excited him that he created an online training school where he could share his passion with others and sell training videos. His father disapproved, not seeing much money in it, but Max persevered while in graduate school as he pursued a degree he hated, but knew was expected of him.

Eventually, he hired consultants to grow and manage his website and soon his business expanded beyond training videos to also include special martial arts equipment, and a line of clothing. He eventually sold the business for several million, which was chump change in his father's eyes, but made Max proud. He'd proven he could be his own man, make his own life, follow his own path.

One woman had proven him wrong. And now Max didn't try to stray too far. He helped his father manage his empire and when, still stinging from his broken engagement, he told his father he was more interested in the security aspect of the clubs than the typical operations, his father conceded and allowed him to study the ins and outs of that industry. That's how Max's present business came to be. MD Defense was a security firm that clients could trust.

Defense was his business. Defense was his creed.

He wouldn't be made a fool of again. He didn't like his friends being used. He had few and treasured the ones he did. This woman had to be stopped.

She *would* be stopped.

He glanced up when he heard footsteps enter the dark paneled room. He looked up at his assistant, Holland, who stood cautiously by the door. He had efficient earnest features like an attentive beagle. But that wasn't why Max trusted him. He'd uncovered the truth about Max's fiancée and had kept the truth to himself since. "You wanted to discuss this week's schedule," he reminded Max.

"Later."

"Has something happened?"

He narrowed his eyes. "Why?"

"You look furious."

He drummed his fingers on the arm of his chair. "I just found out I'm engaged."

"And you didn't know?"

"I didn't even know I was seeing anyone."

"Then how did you get engaged?"

He stared at Holland for a long moment, remembering the last woman to use him. "I'm about to find out." He called James back as a devious idea quickly took formation in his mind and said, "I need you to do me a favor."

*D*esiree couldn't believe the Fortunes were hosting a party and she was invited. She'd never been so excited. She assumed she was going as Rudy's companion so that he wouldn't be overwhelmed by all the guests. She felt honored that they trusted her so much.

The evening James told her, she dashed home to her apartment and looked through the meager offerings of her closet. She didn't want to spend the money she'd made on a dress (she didn't know when her next job would be), but she didn't want to look shabby either. Fortunately, she knew how to sew. She took a simple cotton peach dress from her closet then searched online for a style she could mimic and found one. A sophisticated A-line dress with gold trim and flounced skirt.

Perfect. She bought the accessories at a local craft market and found a closeout sale at a strip mall for some of the extra fabric she'd need. When the day of the event came it brought an early summer breeze and the slow drifting of white clouds. When Rudy saw her, he couldn't stop giggling. At first she worried that he thought her outfit was funny until he told her how pretty she looked and gave her a necklace he'd made.

But the giggling continued.

It had been almost a week and to her relief Rudy had recovered fast from his marriage proposal and the story she'd told him. He'd send her strange looks, but nothing else. But two days ago the secret grins started. He'd look at her and start smiling and she'd ask him why and he'd cover his mouth like a naughty kid and say, "I can't tell you." But by Thursday he was like the cat that'd gotten at the canary.

The day of the party, he took her hand and led her to the back patio where tables and chairs had been expertly set up around the pool and a canopy where a quartet played. Finely dressed guests chatted while attendants met their every need. She saw the Fortunes sitting at the main table. James and Ava, Jackson and Toyin and Edgar. Jackson's wife, Toyin, had come as a bit of a surprise. Desiree had expected more of a model-type fashionista instead of a pretty, full-figured woman with shoulder length black hair that she styled in twists. From what she'd learned, Toyin was a successful businesswoman and artist with a web cartoon growing in popularity. Perhaps Jackson wasn't as superficial as he seemed to be.

And she'd never eaten with Edgar before, a barrel-chested man who had keen, sharp eyes. But today they didn't bother her. For one moment she could pretend that she belonged in this fabulous and elegant world.

It was surreal. She'd tell Million all about it tonight.

James pulled out a chair for her. "You look beautiful," he said.

Jackson studied her. "Where did you get that dress?"

"Connections." She didn't want to tell him that she'd made it herself. She looked around at the crowd. "How often do you do events like this?"

"Not often."

"What's the special occasion?"

"You'll find out," Rudy said in a sing-songy voice.

"W-why the secrecy? What's going on?" She turned to Rudy who continued to have a big grin. "What's so funny?" she asked him. "You have to tell me."

He beamed at her. "You're going to be so happy."

"Happy?"

He nodded. "I asked James to help me make you happy."

"But I am happy."

"No, you're not. You pretend, but you're not. Because of your secret. But now you will be. Now you'll be happy because he's coming."

Desiree's joy slowly turned to dread. "Who's coming?"

"You know," Rudy said then started to giggle.

James sighed. "I'm afraid...we know."

Desiree looked around the table confused, panic slowly starting to grip her. "Know what?" Had they found out about her possible connection to Ava? Had she slipped up somewhere?

"About your boyfriend," Jackson said.

"But I don't—"

"It's too late. Rudy told us everything."

She felt the blood drain from her face.

"I'm sorry I should have warned you," James said. "Rudy doesn't know how to keep secrets."

None of this made sense. What did her stupid secret have to do with them having this event? Slowly, as she put the pieces together, her panic turned into fear. "Wait...did you say he was coming?"

"Yes."

"My fiancé is coming?"

"Yes."

That was impossible. How could her imaginary fiancé be coming to dinner?

"He insisted," James said.

Desiree tapped the table with a trembling finger. "A man is coming here, to your house, to see me?"

"Yes."

Oh no. Oh no! This couldn't be happening. Some crazy person had fooled them. He'd pretended to be her fake fiancé. There was no Maximillian Duchamp. She'd made him up. She'd been specific so that it would be impossible to find him. Now he was coming. He'd *insisted*?

She had to run.

She had to hide.

She had to escape this.

"Don't look like that," Jackson said with a laugh. "We're on your side and we didn't let anyone else know. Nobody here knows about it either. Rudy thought it would be a great surprise. He'd managed to keep it a secret for three whole days which is a record for him."

Rudy smiled at her.

"You shouldn't have," she said in a weak voice. "This is all too much. Rudy, I told you—"

"He's here," Rudy said and she followed his gaze to a man who stood on the balcony overlooking them all. He held a microphone in his hand.

"Thank you all for coming on such short notice," the imposter said in a dark voice that gave her chills. "The Fortunes are hosting, but this little gathering was my idea."

Little gathering? There were nearly fifty people there not including the staff.

Desiree watched the mysterious man, too afraid to move. The voice that carried over the crowd was no voice of some fantasy lover. It was too real, too ominous, too dangerous. She swallowed.

Maybe he was an opportunist who'd thought he'd found a way to blackmail her. He knew the Fortunes had money and he wanted some of it. She didn't know how to stop him.

"Everyone, I have a confession to make," he said. "I don't like keeping secrets from my friends so I thought I should air the truth out here. Ms. Desiree Foster please stand."

She swallowed hard again. She'd endure this until she could tell the Fortunes in private that she'd lied. She rose to her feet.

"Thank you." He walked down the balcony stairs. "I know this must be a surprise to you. It was a surprise to me too. I wanted to have my friends around to meet you."

She watched him come closer to her. That's when

she realized he didn't have the eyes of a greedy opportunist; he didn't smile like a man who wanted to pretend to be engaged.

He had the eyes of an assassin.

And he looked ready to kill her.

CHAPTER 18

He turned his back to her and addressed the crowd. "Everyone I want you to know that I am not, nor will I ever be, engaged to this woman."

She wanted to fall into the ground. Be swallowed whole and buried.

"I want you all to be careful of this scheming, duplicitous woman. To have her face imprinted in your brains so that you won't fall prey to her lies."

James jumped to his feet. "Max, this isn't funny. I know how private you are. If you're angry because she made a simple mistake of telling us—"

Max shifted his hard gaze to James. "I am telling you, that I've never met this woman in my life. I've never spoken to her. I have no idea who she is or why she gave you my name or how she could know so much about me. I give her credit." He pinned Desiree with a look that made her feel like an insect fastened to a corkboard with a pin through its abdomen. "She did a thorough research but you made a mistake. You didn't know I'd be in town early did you? You thought you'd be gone by then? How much were you hoping to make?"

They all looked at her.

Desiree could feel every gaze on her. He'd publically branded her a liar, a schemer, an outsider. He'd shamed her and, worst of all, he'd shamed her in front of Ava. Now she felt the weight of her handmade dress, cheap jewelry, that she'd had more jobs than the four of them combined even though she was younger than them. Ava was the golden beauty and she was the pathetic loser.

"Desiree," James said in an urgent voice. "Tell me what's going on."

She felt the gathering of tears. She hated being humiliated in front of Ava but what hurt most was disappointing James and Rudy. "I didn't mean to lie."

"Then why did you?"

She shook her head. "I'm sorry."

"Sorry you got caught," Max said in disgust. "Don't let the tears fool you. I've seen that act before. I'm just sorry that she'd stoop so low as to use Rudy—"

Desiree felt her shame turn into anger. This man could accuse her of many things, but never of deliberately hurting Rudy. She held up her hand. "Stop right there."

The corner of his mouth quirked. "Did I touch a nerve?"

"You're a monster. You weren't even supposed to exist. I made you up. I made everything up."

"You used my name."

"It wasn't supposed to be *you!*"

"Why?" James asked. "Why did you lie?"

"Because..." She looked at Rudy's stunned expression then turned away. "I didn't want to..." She shook her head. "I can't tell you right now."

"But you will," Max said, his voice a command. "I think we all have a right to know why you lied. No more secrets."

She bit her lip. She hated this man. She didn't know how he could possibly be Maximillian Duchamp but she hated him with a passion that poured acid in her veins. He meant to destroy her, but she wouldn't let him. He hated her too for some unknown reason, but that didn't matter. She'd been hated before. She could stand it. Her tears dried up and her voice lost its tremble. He wanted pain. She'd give him buckets of it. But not at Rudy's expense.

"I'll tell you everything inside, but not out here," she said in a low voice. "It's about Rudy."

James took the hint and said to the crowd, "We apologize. We have a delicate family emergency to deal with. There are special gifts for you as you leave." He motioned to one of the staff who nodded, letting him know everything would be taken care of. He then rested his hand on the base of Desiree's back and hustled her inside. "This had better be good," he said in a low warning.

And behind her she heard Jackson say to Max, "You could have handled this better," and Max replied, "I may be single, but do I look desperate?" which made her hate him more. Not only did he need to humiliate her but he had to insult her as well?

Minutes later they all gathered in the great room. Max stood to the side while everyone else sat, except for

Desiree who stood too and faced them as if she were a criminal sent to the gallows and offered a last plea to save her life. "Okay, I lied," she said. "I lied because I didn't want to hurt Rudy's feelings when he asked me to marry him. I didn't want to reject the beautiful ring he'd made for me so I came up with a name and a man. I lied because I didn't want to lose this job. I need this job. I know that's something you wouldn't understand because making money comes easy to you, but others like me have to hustle every day. I couldn't even afford to buy a new dress, I had to redesign this old dress from my wardrobe.

"I lied because I not only wanted to protect Rudy's feelings and liked and needed this job but because my mother thinks that Ava is her long-lost daughter and I wanted to pretend just for a moment that I could measure up. Yes, I used a name and I am so sorry," she briefly looked at Max, "it was your name. I did because if I'd had to come up with a real man to pretend to be my fiancé you can be assured I'd *never* think of you. You're the last man I'd ever want to be connected to even in passing."

The assassin's gaze didn't change, but he looked a little less certain.

She turned to James and Rudy. "I can't apologize enough..." But her words fell away when she realized that James wasn't looking at her, he was sharing a look with his brother.

"That's it," Jackson said.

James nodded. "A family resemblance."

She didn't know what they were talking about. They couldn't think she looked anything like Ava.

"You know my mother?" Ava said.

"Who the hell are you?" Edgar demanded.

"I gave you my real name," Desiree said. "My mother is Lida Foster. She saw Ava's picture on the TV while in the hospital and told me some story about her daughter Amelia and her ex-husband Walter Bremmer. I didn't give it much thought, but I was curious. More like my mother was curious. She wanted to know as much about Ava as she could before she met her again. And she was afraid that her ex might have said lies about her. Meeting Rudy and James on the street was purely accidental, I was heading towards his shop but that was all and then when James gave me a chance to work here, I thought I could find out more about Ava on my own without anyone else knowing. I was going to tell you. I'm sure it doesn't make any sense to you. I'm not after your money. I know it must sound crazy about a kid being stolen at three years old and—"

"It's true," Ava said in a quiet voice.

"What?"

"My real name is Amelia. I only found that out recently and my father changed his name from Walter Bremmer."

Edgar shook his head. "Lida...after all these years. Why didn't she call me?"

"She knows you?" Desiree said.

He nodded. "Used to work for me. Over the years we lost touch, but I never thought it would come to this."

"She didn't mention you. But she seemed really afraid of this Walter guy."

"She had a right to," Edgar said.

Desiree sank into a seat. Her mother wasn't delusional. It was all true. She was actually related to this woman? "Oh."

"You said she's in the hospital?"

"She's better now. It was a bad reaction to a new prescription."

"Does she have other children...besides you?" Ava asked.

"Just my brother. Uh...our brother. Laurence. He's a ... He can't wait to meet you."

"I don't know what to say."

Ava looked so devastated that Desiree got over her humiliation and felt a little sorry for her. Hugging her would be out of the question. She didn't look like the touchy-feely type and shaking hands didn't seem rational either. Plus, in truth, she was still scared of her, too scared to get close. "I know it's a lot to take in. Mom knows I'm here, but I told her I wouldn't tell you anything until after the eight weeks were over." She shot a look at Max. The jerk had ruined everything. She'd been so close to revealing the truth when she felt ready. "But since things have changed, I can—"

"Not yet. Not yet." Ava said almost in a panic. "Don't tell her anything yet. Excuse me." She fled from the room.

James pointed at Desiree. "Stay here. Don't make me find you," he said, then followed Ava.

"You lied to me," Rudy said. "I don't like friends who lie." He raced from the room.

Edgar gestured to Toyin. "Go check on the guests. I

don't want any stragglers." Before she could protest, he shifted his gaze to Jackson. "You. Follow me."

Desiree watched the last three lines of defense walk out of the room.

Leaving her alone with her worst nightmare.

CHAPTER 19

*H*e was everything she couldn't stand in a man. He was too tall, too broadly built, like he could crack nuts with his thumb, he had no refinement or elegance at all. He had a dark mustache to match his dark brows and lashes. She couldn't stand a mustache. He was also too rich, she wouldn't even try to price how much his black suit or Italian shoes cost, let alone the diamond in his ear. Next to him, Jackson looked like he'd shopped at a bargain basement store.

Max folded his arms. "You're a real troublemaker."

"Describing what you are would be a waste of breath. Is this how you treat your friends? By humiliating them? I can understand you wanting to get back at me, although I don't understand why you had to do it on such a grand scale, unless your insecurity complex is beyond measure, but you gave them no warning."

"I did it to protect them."

"From what? You could have told them over the phone, you could have—"

"Been quiet and polite so that you could manipulate them in secret? Secrets like to thrive in darkness, I prefer to bring things to light where they will shrivel and die."

"Did it even once cross your mind that I might have lied to protect someone too? Did you see Rudy's face? That was your fault not mine."

"No, I wasn't the one who lied to him. I have nothing to hide."

"And you're a jerk. Couldn't you have pretended?"

He blinked bored. "Why would I do that? What would I get out of it?"

"I told you that it had nothing to do with you. I hurt a kind man's feelings. Or didn't you notice?"

"Rudy's right. You shouldn't have lied to him. Lesson learned. That's your fault not mine."

She turned.

"James told you not to go anywhere."

"Are you going to stop me?"

"Take one more step and you'll find out."

Desiree glared at him then sat and stared at one of the large windows. "I should have called him Maxwell."

"Who?"

"My imaginary fiancé."

"You're still going to stick to your story that you described me by accident?"

"Yes. I didn't describe *you* at all." She turned to him stunned. "You still think I'm lying?"

"You knew too much about me for it to be coincidence."

"It was. A horrible coincidence. Like being hit by lighting on your wedding day. Like finding out your boyfriend is actually your brother."

"That's not a coincidence that's a—"

"I don't care. I don't care what you think about me. All I care about is how I'm going to fix this." She jumped to her feet. She didn't care if he tried to stop her. She headed for the stairs.

He blocked her path, moving with such speed that she actually bumped into him. "Where are you going?"

She rubbed her forehead. "You're like a brick wall."

"Where are you going?"

She took a step back. "I'm not leaving the house if that's what you're wondering."

"Answer the question."

"I have to talk to Rudy. Am I allowed to do that?"

He nodded. "Sure."

It took her a second to realize what he was up to. "You're going to follow me?"

"Until James has a chance to talk to you, I'm not leaving your side."

"I'd rather have thrush." She moved to the side.

He blocked her again. "Do you want to talk to Rudy or not?"

She sighed. "Fine." When he let her pass, she said, "I want to talk with him alone." She headed up the stairs.

"Of course you do."

"I mean it. Stay away. You've upset him enough."

"Funny how you keep trying to blame me for being a liar."

"I'm not a—forget it." When she reached the second

floor she headed down the hall then stopped in front of a door. She knocked. "Rudy? Can I talk to you?"

She heard no reply.

She turned the knob, glad it wasn't locked. She opened the door, walked inside and started to close it. Max held the door, stopping her. She could feel his strength, knowing she couldn't win against him. She looked at him startled by his insistence. Was this guy for real?

"Leave it open," he said.

"But—"

"I won't come inside, but leave the door open."

She released the door handle, gripping her hand into a fist. He was a big, bully.

"And talk loud enough so that I can hear what you're saying," he added with a smile as if he took pleasure in her anger.

"It's a private conversation."

"Not anymore."

"Do you enjoy being a complete a—"

"Yes." He shoved her forward. "Now go before James returns downstairs and wonders where we are." If James had followed Ava to one of the upstairs rooms, the long hallway had two ways one could take to the lower level so James could return to the great room without passing him.

She'd never loathed someone so much in her entire life, but arguing with him would take up too much time and she had to focus on Rudy.

She entered his room, a place she'd grown familiar with, but now made her feel like an intruder, and saw him sitting at his desk, which was stacked with books, papers and his laptop. He kept his back to her. "I hate to barge in like this but I need to talk to you." She sat on the bed. "I'm really sorry. I know lying to you was wrong."

"I know why you lied. You lied because you didn't want to marry somebody like me."

"No, I turned you down because I don't...I don't love you enough to want to marry you. I lied because I didn't want to hurt your feelings. And I wanted you to be impressed."

He turned around and frowned. "Impressed?"

She hesitated, knowing her words would be overheard, but it was time to be truthful and she couldn't care what the bully at the door would think. "I wanted to belong. You have accomplished so much. You have a business, you have lots of friends, you're getting college credits. I haven't managed half of that so I wanted to tell you a story that made me look better. I wanted you to think that I was somebody special."

He didn't respond.

"I won't make up a story like that again. Truly."

He lowered his head.

She waited for him to ask her why not, but he remained silent. "You'll make a good husband to someone else."

He still didn't look at her.

"Can we be friends again?"

"Are you really poor?"

"Poor?"

"You said you needed the money."

"Oh, that...you don't have to worry about that. I was

only trying to explain why I...no I'm not poor. I'm just between jobs at the moment. And I really like this one and hope I can stay. Can I?"

He hesitated. "I'm still mad at you."

"That's okay. You can be mad at friends even after you forgive them."

"You made James mad too."

Desiree sighed. "I know. I'll talk to him later."

"He can stay mad a long time."

"I hope not too long. Friends again?"

He nodded. "Only if James says so."

Damn. After Max, facing James was one of the last things she wanted to do.

CHAPTER 20

She couldn't believe this was happening. Ava paced her bedroom, trying to get her breathing under control. She wasn't ready. Her mother had seen her on television? Had known her by sight? She had a half-sister and brother?

"Ava?"

She took a deep breath then turned to James who stood in the bedroom doorway. "I'm alright. You don't have to worry about me. I'm sorry I ran out of the room like that. Is she okay?"

James stepped into the room and closed the door behind him. His eyes didn't leave her face and his voice was soft when he spoke. "Ava."

The sound of her name on his lips opened up something deep within her. Something that scared her. She looked at his big brown form and he was her Douglas fir tree and she wanted to climb him like a black bear. Claw her way to the top and wrap her legs around him. She wanted to feel his hot flesh next to hers. She wanted to feel only that...nothing else. She walked up to him and rested a hand on his chest. "I'm glad to have you alone. You look good."

He sighed. "Ava." This time when he said her name it wasn't a question or a plea it sounded sad.

She sniffed his neck then touched it with the tip of her tongue. "I want you."

James drew back. "You don't have to pretend—"

"I'm not pretending." She closed the tiny distance between them. "Wouldn't this be fun? Exciting. To see how fast we can do this before people start wondering about us?"

He didn't move. She wanted him to reach for her, she wanted his mouth on hers, his body close. Her eagerness, desperation, grew as the seconds passed, as he continued to study her. She needed him to play along. She needed him to follow her lead. She smiled. "Come on, James." She took his arms and wrapped them around her. "I want you to hold me tight. No, tighter than that. Much tighter. I want you to hold me so tight that you could crack a rib."

His voice deepened. "I'm not going to do that."

"I need this. I want this. Please. I need a little pain. You know I do. I don't ask you to do this often. Just this once. It can be quick. Punch me in the hip. The fleshy part. I can take it." When she felt him stiffen she quickly said, "It's not abuse if I ask you to do it. You know me. You know what I like."

He slowly shook his head.

She pushed him away in disgust. "Why must you be such a coward?"

He turned his face away, but kept the rest of his body facing her, his hands on his hips. The portrait of a man gaining control of himself. But she didn't want him in control, she wanted to push him. She needed his heat to bury her dark fears.

"If you don't want to, I can always find someone else willing."

He didn't move, not right away, but she felt the air go cold and for a second she wondered if she'd pushed him too far. Then, with the patience of a practiced predator, he slowly turned his gaze to hers. Before she could say anything else, he launched at her with such speed that she cried out in alarm. He grabbed her wrist in a viselike grip and shoved her against the wall, with such force that it hurt, which terrified and thrilled her. His eyes were onyx. "This is what you want from me?" he ground out between clenched teeth. "You want to make me angry enough to hurt you?"

Ava licked her lower lip. "You know it turns me on. Be rough, be wild, I like it."

"I can be rough, you know I can, but you're asking me to be brutal. You're asking me to cross the line. And that's never going to happen." He released her wrist and bit his lip. "Now...let's talk about what just happened."

Ava gripped the front of his shirt in her fists, her body shaking. "Don't you get it? I don't want to talk! I don't want...I want you. I need you to...I'm asking, begging you to—" She couldn't say it. All she felt was too hard to put into words. She shoved him away in disgust. She couldn't stand how vulnerable he made her feel. "What is wrong with you? What's so hard to understand? I don't want your tender touch and understanding gaze. I don't want you sitting in front of me ready to listen to my feelings. Your compassion makes me sick. I hate it. I hate when you hold me close like some treasure you found, I hate the light touch of your fingers on my forehead, the touch of your lips on my cheek. I don't want that kind of man. Especially not now. I want a powerful man, who treats me like a powerful woman. Who does what I say without fear."

James nodded then wrapped his hand around her throat and whispered in a velvet tone, "It won't work, my love. You can't push me to lose control. I promised myself I'd never touch you in anger and that's one promise I don't intend to break." He left the room.

Ava sunk down on the bed. She wished he understood. She needed to hurt, she needed pain to stop the aching inside. What if she wasn't good enough? What if her mother ended up disappointed? What if she couldn't relate to her new family? It had always been just her father and her and with him out of her life now...she'd be reminded of what she'd lost. The years she'd lost. How would it feel to see what it might have been like growing up with a mother?

Desiree always seemed so sunny and cheerful, she envied her. She couldn't come close to being that optimistic about life. What if her mother expected her to be the same? Not so serious, not so cerebral.

She closed her eyes, fighting against tears and hugged herself, wishing she hadn't driven James away. She needed an outlet for this rising pain, this swelling ache. She bit her lip, hard enough to draw blood. She dragged her nails down her arm. But it wasn't enough. The pain still lingered. She glanced at the closed door to make sure it was firmly shut before she got on her knees and slid her hand between the mattress and the frame. When her hand wrapped around a wooden handle she grinned and pulled out the knife she'd hidden there. She'd hidden it deep enough so that the staff couldn't see it when they changed the sheets. She held up the paring knife, seeing part of her reflection in the steel blade. It would be perfect.

She'd hidden it there for times like this. She hadn't had to use it in the past, her new life with the Fortunes hadn't warranted that, but now she needed it. She went into the bathroom and locked the door. She sat on the edge of the bathtub and placed the knife against her skin.

The moment it pierced her flesh she felt a sense of relief, even as the sight of blood broke free and slid down her arm and dropped on the floor. She closed her eyes. She could do this. She could handle this. She could be in control.

James didn't understand. She didn't want to be loved right now. Not when she was so afraid. Not when she felt so unlovable. Even though her mother wanted to meet her, she had another life that Ava wasn't sure she could be a part of. What if she didn't get on with her siblings? She was so used to being on her own. Even getting used to how the Fortunes did things had taken an adjustment. How could she make another one? The price was even higher. She had to belong. She had to prove her father wrong, that she was her own woman. And she hated the thought of disappointing James. Of failing him. Of not being the woman he'd thought he'd married.

She made another thin slice with the knife, then slid to the cold tiled floor and rested her head against the cool rim of the bathtub, while she kept her arm in place so that any blood would fall into the tub and be easily washed away.

She'd endured worse. She'd endured her father's anger and lies. She could endure this.

Once she felt the internal ache subside she opened her eyes and cleaned up both the blood and the wound. She couldn't wear a bandage that would be too obvious and James would ask questions, but a bracelet would cover up a band aid, which she took out of the medicine cabinet.

She was certain she'd gotten the bleeding to stop, but she couldn't take any risks. She searched through her jewelry until she found one that was just the right shape and size.

She slid it on, ready to face what was coming.

CHAPTER 21

Max always wondered how a man could smile and still look like he wanted to ring your neck. James managed the expression perfectly when he came down the hall and found Max leaning against the wall outside of Rudy's bedroom. James started to say something, but stopped when Desiree came out of the room and looked at him startled.

"I was just talking to Rudy," she said like a guilty prisoner caught by a warden.

He nodded.

"I kept an eye on her," Max said, but the look James gave him made it clear he wasn't grateful.

He patted him on the shoulder. "I need to talk to you." He looked at Desiree. "I'll talk to you later."

She held up her hands as if he'd pointed a gun at her. "Don't worry, I'm not leaving."

He nodded again then headed down the hall,

expecting Max to follow, which he did at a more leisurely pace.

He had no regrets. Sure, he could have handle things differently. He could have gone along with Desiree's little lie to see where it might lead, but that wasn't who he was. He detested liars. He'd wanted to see one in action and take her down.

He may be used to people using him, using his connections, but this was a first. Someone using his name and pretending to have a connection that could be easily checked. He didn't like liars, but dumb liars were the worst. He found them abhorrent.

She surprised him. She didn't look stupid. She didn't look much of anything if he were being really honest. If he were being generous—which he rarely found a reason to be-he'd say she was pretty. Not striking, not a head turner, but she had features that had been put together nicely. She was on the chubby side and not particularly tall.

But he wasn't in a generous mood so all he saw was a mischievous woman with sharp eyes and a too easy grin. It was probably that grin that had fooled the Fortunes. They were usually sharper with who they let into their inner circle, especially who they let around their susceptible brother.

He wondered which brother she'd used those brown eyes and easy smile on first. Jackson. Had to be Jackson. He was known for his women troubles...but how she'd been able to also fool James amazed him.

But after overhearing her conversation with Rudy, Max knew how dangerous she was. How she'd tricked one of them. If he wasn't sharper he would have believed her too. She sounded so sincere. He was reluctantly impressed.

But she'd taken her little game too far. She'd encountered the master hunter of liars and cheats. He would not be one of her victims.

He followed James into the library, a place that impressed him. It actually had books. His family home had bookshelves filled with statues, awards, and photographs but few books. He walked to a chair and started to sit when James said, "Stand."

He paused surprised and looked at him. "What?"

"Don't sit down. You might not be here that long."

Whoa. James was angrier than he'd thought. He might have miscalculated a little. "Listen."

"What the hell were you thinking? You asked me to host a party for you for a woman you've never met?"

"I wanted to expose her. Women like that thrive in secret and—"

"You have no idea what your little ploy nearly cost us. Nobody but the family knows about Ava's background, about her parent's divorce, and what happened after."

"I didn't expect that," Max said with regret. "But are you sure you can believe that story about her mother?"

James rubbed his eyes. "Yes. I told you. She knows things few outside the family do."

"Doesn't matter, she knew things about me too. She could be a professional at this. Trust me I've been conned before."

James shook his head. "She isn't like that."

"You don't know." He gestured to the door. "Look at

all that you didn't know about her. That was after a background check. You better be careful. That bi—"

James pointed at him. "She's family so watch what you say."

"Until you get a DNA test, I wouldn't make that claim."

"Edgar recognized her mother's name."

"Names are easy. She could have done her research. How can you fall for her lies?"

"She didn't lie. Besides, she reminds me of Ava. From the first moment there was something about her I couldn't put my finger on. Certain looks and gestures. I can't explain it, but Jackson sensed it too. She's the real deal. I believe her story. I think she made a mistake using your name, I don't think she's dangerous."

"She lied about being engaged."

"And you betrayed me."

Max blinked stunned.

"Do you have any idea of what you've done? You embarrassed me in front of Edgar." He pounded his chest with his fist. "You disgraced a guest in *my* home, you caused my wife pain."

"I thought—"

"You weren't thinking at all. You could have told me over the phone. You could have shared your concerns and suspicions because that's what friends do. They don't plan a surprise attack behind their back."

Max shoved his hands into his pockets. "I'm sorry. It's just—" He stopped. He didn't want to offer excuses or tell him the reason why he'd been so afraid for them. That he'd been a victim of a woman's lies that had done a lot of damage not just to him but to the people he cared about. But he'd met the Fortunes after that debacle and didn't wish to share his private shame. "I was wrong. How can I make it up to you?"

"Apologize to her."

He rubbed his chin. "Are you sure Ava's ready to see me right now?"

James shook his head. "Not Ava. Desiree."

Max laughed.

James didn't smile.

Max narrowed his eyes. "Absolutely not. She lied. I exposed her. End of story."

"She explained why."

Max's brows shot up. "I don't care."

"She made a mistake. She didn't want to hurt Rudy's feelings and I understand that. You're the one who blew this out of proportion."

"She's the one who made up a story about being engaged to me."

"It wasn't her fault that Rudy told us."

"What if that was part of her plan?"

"Now you're starting to sound paranoid."

He had his reasons. "I think you're taking this a little too casually."

"And I think you're taking this a little too seriously."

"It's not over yet, she'll ask for money. Just wait. I should—"

"You have five seconds to decide. Do you want to leave this house as friends or enemies?"

Max spun away from him wanting to break something. The woman was going to win. Liars always knew how to plant seeds of dissension. He didn't want to lose his friendship because of her. That's how they gained strength—divide and conquer. He had to stay close to keep an eye on her. His friend could still be in danger and not know it. "I'll apologize for the party, but that's all."

James nodded. "Fine."

Max pulled out his cell phone. "What's her number?"

James frowned. "You're not apologizing by text."

"Fine. Flowers then."

"Nope."

Max looked at him in surprise, as if his friend had asked him to do something obscene. "You expect me to do it in person?"

"You owe her that much."

"I'll send chocolates too. Chubby girls tend to like sweet things."

James folded his arms.

Max swore. "I don't believe this."

"After I've finished talking to Desiree, you're going to say you're sorry and mean it. That's the deal."

Max swore again with more feeling, rubbing the back of his neck. "Man, this woman is good. I feared as much."

"I mean it."

"I know." He cleared his throat. "I'm truly sorry if I hurt Ava in any way."

"Unfortunately, meeting Desiree may be exactly what she needs."

CHAPTER 22

A crushed rose, a butterfly that had been stepped on.

That was what Desiree reminded James of when he found her in the garden. It had taken him awhile to find her there. He'd searched the house and it was only after asking one of the staff where she was that's he'd managed to find her. She held her head down. From the corner of his eye he could see catering staff removing the table and chairs and the rest of the remnants of the ruined party as the dying sunlight melted into the petals and leaves of the garden.

He was half-surprised that she hadn't disappeared. Part of him wished she had then he wouldn't have to face her now. After dealing with Ava and Max he felt emotionally exhausted. But his sense of duty gave him strength.

He took the seat in front of her. "Why didn't you tell me?"

She lifted her head and looked so miserable that he couldn't be angry at her. He knew Max would think he was crazy to believe her, but he did. Wholeheartedly. He didn't think her helping Rudy had been a ploy, she'd been genuine. He believed her about lying to Rudy to spare his feelings. No one else had paid much attention to Rudy's reaction to his girlfriend's breakup. He'd been crushed and racing into the road to get her to notice him had only been a symptom of his lingering heartache. The incident hadn't been and couldn't have been manipulated.

He believed Desiree that Rudy had asked her to marry him. It was something he would do. Impulsively? Absolutely. Rudy didn't like everybody. That made James trust her. He didn't think she was out to hurt them, to hurt anyone, even though she had.

He nodded to her chair. "That used to be my mother's favorite spot."

Desiree jumped up, alarmed. "I'm sorry, I didn't know—"

"No," he said quickly. "It's okay. It's not a shrine or anything. I just thought you should know. It's...it's nice to see you there. This garden was her baby."

"It's beautiful."

"She gone now, but when I'm here..."

"It's comforting." She hung her head again. "I don't know what to say."

"I think you've already said a lot."

"Do you want me to leave?"

"I want to understand."

"I'm not a liar. I don't know what your friend told you, but—"

"I believe you."

Her head snapped up. She looked at him with such hope and joy that he couldn't stop a smile.

"Really?"

"Yes."

She blinked back tears, relieved. "It wasn't supposed to happen like this." She shook her head. "We—I—don't want money. My mother only recently told me this crazy story about her daughter being kidnapped by her ex-husband and some wealthy man trying to help her find her and the years that she's been searching. I mean, one moment she's in the hospital nearly being put in the psych ward, and the next she's telling me about her daughter getting stolen."

"It's all true."

"I was afraid of that."

"Why?"

She shrugged. "I don't know. Because it changes everything. I thought I knew my mother and now I don't. I don't know this woman who had an entire life that I never knew about. I'm scared to accept this."

"You're not the only one."

"Ava feels the same?" Desiree said amazed.

James nodded. He looked tired and sad, but the expression was so brief she wasn't sure she'd seen it. She hated the thought that she'd caused him pain or any problems in their marriage.

"Why? She has nothing to worry about. Mom will adore her. Laurence will too. She has no idea how excited they both are to meet her. And Mom wants to know everything about her."

"But now you know it's true that you're related. How do you feel?"

"My mother will be ecstatic."

"What about you?"

"It doesn't matter what I think."

He narrowed his eyes a fraction but didn't respond.

"I'm happy I found her."

"Are you worried about your mother?"

"Worried?"

"You mentioned this last hospital visit and then that she started a gas stove fire."

"Oh, well...she has her moments, but she's not mentally unstable if that's what you're wondering."

He sensed she was holding something back but didn't press her. "I'm going to take the lead on this. I want you to call your mother. Tell her that we'll take care of any arrangements she needs."

"Okay."

"You can contact your brother too."

"Okay."

"Is there anything else I should know?"

"No, that's it. Unless..."

"Unless what?"

"If you want me to give you a DNA sample I'm willing. Just to make sure."

"I told you I believe you. It's not something anyone else knows about Ava."

"But I'd hate for my mother to be wrong."

"Everything can be easily confirmed. I have a picture of Ava's father, if he's the man your mother was married to and divorced she'd know, plus Edgar also knew your mother. That's enough for me. If you have a picture of her, I can show him."

"It's been more than thirty years."

"People don't change that much." He paused. "You don't want this to be true, do you?"

She slowly shook her head. "It's not that. My mother can be a dreamer. I don't want her to get her hopes up and then find out...why are you smiling?"

"You're more like your sister than you think. I don't know why you're both so nervous about this."

It was strange to have him so casually refer to Ava as her sister and she couldn't imagine them having anything in common. "I'm just being cautious. Plus I want to prove Max wrong. Science is evidence."

"Understood. If it makes you feel better, we'll get a test done. There are labs that can get a result in one or two days. But the one I want to use is top of the line and thorough. It's expensive and the results will take about two to three weeks. Is that okay?"

"Yes. Thank you."

James was silent for a moment then said, "How's Rudy?"

"Still mad at me, but I told him how sorry I am."

James nodded. "That's enough. By tomorrow you'll be in his good graces again. He's not one to hold a grudge."

"How about your...friend?"

The corner of his mouth kicked up then he pulled out his phone and sent a text. "Max has something to say to you." He stood.

"Where are you going?"

"I think this should be between the two of you."

She surged to her feet, clasping her hands together in a plea. "I already said I was sorry."

"I know. You won't have to say anything, he'll—"

She grabbed his sleeve like a child afraid to be left alone in the dark. "Please don't leave me alone with him again. I've been punished enough."

"Don't look at me like that. He's not going to hurt you."

"Again," she said in a flat tone.

James sent her a long look. "Did he say anything else—"

"No, but please don't go."

"All right. I'll—"

The sound of footsteps stopped his words. Max paused surprised to see James still there. James nodded. "Go on."

Desiree watched Max's expression as she stood behind James.

It was probably wrong to have a crush on one's brother-in- law, but Desiree couldn't help herself. When she saw Max's cynical expression waver at the sight of James her heart soared. Here he had a worthy opponent, he couldn't bully her. And James had stayed, protecting her from this awful man. She could have hugged him.

Max shifted his gaze from James to hers. "I apologize."

"For what?" James pressed.

Max's gaze hardened. James stared back unfazed. Max sighed. "For embarrassing my friends...and you. And that's all I'll say, understood?"

James nodded.

Max sent her one last glare then left.

"Feel better?"

Desiree resisted the childish urge to pick up a rock and throw it at the back of Max's head. "He's annoyed that anyone would even think he'd stoop so low to be engaged to someone like me."

"You overheard that?"

"He didn't exactly whisper it."

James hesitated. "Don't form too quick an opinion, you're seeing him at his worse."

"I hope to never see him again."

CHAPTER 23

That evening as the sun settled firmly behind the horizon James sat alone in the great room, trying to focus on data he'd been given but failing. Although Jackson had talked to Edgar and tried to smooth things over, his stepfather was still angered by James's blunder. Whether it was hiring Desiree without more due diligence or hosting a party for Max without discovering his real motive, he didn't know. He didn't blame his stepfather for being upset with him.

When he heard someone sniff above him, he looked up from his laptop and saw Rudy. His heart broke. His brother looked miserable.

"Did you talk to Desiree?" he asked, already knowing the answer.

He nodded.

"Did she apologize?"

He nodded once more.

"Did you forgive her?"

He nodded a third time and wiped his eyes.

"But you're still sad?"

Rudy's face fell and the tears flowed. James motioned him forward. Rudy sat down beside him and James rubbed his cheek. "I'm sorry," he said then hugged him.

"I loved her and wanted her to marry me."

He drew back and wiped his brother's tears. "I know."

"But she doesn't love me and doesn't want to marry me. Do you think anyone will want to marry me?"

"I don't know, but you know that we love you. And Desiree cares about you in her own way. Friendship is a different kind of love and sometimes longer lasting."

Rudy hung his head. "Still hurts."

"Getting your feelings hurt is part of life."

"I like her so much. She reminds me of Mom."

James nodded, feeling a lump in his throat. That was it. That was also why Desiree felt so familiar. She reminded him of the bright light that had filled the house when his mother was alive. She made them all feel so good when they were around her. He didn't blame Rudy for falling for her so fast. Unlike Max, James knew that Desiree was special. A real genuine light who had entered their lives.

"Do you want me to send her away so you can work with someone else?" It would be hard to get someone suitable at such short notice, but he'd manage.

Rudy shook his head. "I don't want her to go away." He looked up at him. "But you're sad too."

James forced a reluctant smile. "I'm sad for another reason."

"Why?"

James looked away, he couldn't share all that weighed on his heart. How he felt that he hadn't protected his family. He felt like he'd let down Edgar by threatening the reputation of their family name, he'd let down Ava by not finding out more about Desiree, he'd let down Desiree by exposing her to Max's anger. It was too much to think about. "I'm sad because when you hurt, I hurt."

Rudy sniffed and wiped his eyes. "I'm sorry. I'll try not to be sad anymore."

James patted him on the back and sighed. "Me too."

THE NEXT MORNING, Desiree saw Ava sprawled on the sectional in the great room reading a comic book of some sort and approached her like she would a panther.

"I wanted to apologize."

"It's okay," Ava said, without lifting her head. "You've already done that."

"I spoke to James and..." She cautiously took a seat at the base of her feet, careful not to touch her. "...this isn't his fault. I'd hate for you to be mad at him."

She lifted her head. "Why would you think I was mad at him?"

"He looked sad."

Ava tensed, her tone turned cold. "Do you think you know my husband better than I do?"

Desiree jerked back as if she'd been slapped. "No, I—"

Ava flashed a smile that didn't reach her eyes. "Good,

I would hate for us to have that misunderstanding no matter how good your intentions."

"Right."

She returned her attention to her book. "We may be related, but it doesn't mean you can start giving me advice."

"Right."

James came into the room walked up behind Ava and bent towards her to place a kiss on her cheek then hesitated and stopped. Desiree could understand his hesitation, she'd sooner place her lips on the head of a viper.

"Am I interrupting anything?" he said.

"No," Ava said before Desiree could speak.

Desiree hesitated wondering whether she should stay or go. The tension in the air hovered, thick and dense like a fog over a swamp, and she didn't know what to do.

She felt slightly ill, as if she'd gotten punched in the gut. She'd known that Ava was a hard woman to know, but she didn't expect her to be so cold. How could James have ended up with a woman like that? The flashing expression of sadness and tiredness she'd seen on his face in the garden came and went again. Something was different between them.

But she couldn't read Ava's expression, it was too guarded.

"What's with the tension in here?" Jackson said, strolling into the room, putting voice to Desiree's thoughts.

"Leave it," James said. He picked up a book from the coffee table. A hardcover book that looked like a thriller from the glint of a knife image on the cover.

"You look like hell." Jackson sent Ava a glance. "You torturing him again? Making him regret taking my place?"

James shot his brother a look. "I said leave it."

Jackson shoved his hands in his pockets, unfazed by his brother's warning. He turned to Desiree. "Have any more secrets you want to share?"

Ava closed her book and looked at him. "What are you doing here? Did Toyin toss you out because she finally realized she married a boy instead of a man?"

Jackson's expression darkened.

Desiree jumped to her feet. "Don't do this. Don't fight. I don't know what's going on, but I know it's my fault because—"

"It's not your fault," Ava cut in. "Jackson likes to push buttons like a bored little child. Especially when it comes to us." Ava rose to her feet and patted him on the cheek. "But I'm not in the mood to play today." She turned to Desiree. "I'm leaving. I suggest you do the same."

Desiree watched her go, her heart racing. She glanced at James who nodded, encouraging her to leave as well. Once both women had left the room he turned to his brother and said, "What's with you?"

"I could ask you the same. I thought Ava wanted to meet her mother, what's with the attitude?"

James set the book back down. "It's complicated."

"It seems simple to me. What is she doing to you?"

"Nothing."

"You look like you haven't slept."

"I was up late working."

"On what?"

"You've never asked before. What makes you so curious now? What are you doing here?"

"Edgar wanted to see me about something."

"What?"

Jackson flashed a smile and repeated his brother's words. "You've never asked before. What makes you so curious now?"

"Ava's right. You need to grow up."

His smile fell. "You know I hate when you take her side against me."

"And you know I hate when you remind me how our marriage started. Because you dumped her at the altar."

"I told you I was—"

"Doesn't matter."

Jackson swore. "I don't like what's going on. Something's not right about all this."

"You don't believe Desiree's story?"

"No, it's not that. It's how she and Ava are both stalling to have this reunion. Don't you think that's strange?"

James rested his hands on his hips and nodded. "What I think is that we all need a break."

CHAPTER 24

*B*itchhhhhhhh! I hate youuuuuu!

Desiree closed her eyes as her car speakers blasted the rock singer's words. She'd found refuge in her car after leaving James and Jackson to their argument about Ava.

Ava.

Everything was about Ava.

Youuuu ruined my liiiiiife!!

The brush of the early summer sun hid behind a series of dark, grey clouds, making the day feel like it was on the verge of night. It felt perfect for her escape. She drove down to the end of the drive letting the Fortune house glare down at her from a distance. Her car was her safe place. She found sanctuary in it. In her hard rock music. She put it on loud and sang at the top of her voice. She loved the screaming voices, the wail of an electric guitar and heavy drumbeats that threatened to knock her out of her seat like a sonic boom. The music had helped her from middle school until now. When she would lock herself away in her room, put her headphones on and jump around, sometimes lifting her hands in the air and bobbing her head. When she'd gotten her first car—a ten year old Toyota with a back window that wouldn't work—it became her haven.

Like now. Especially now.

She bobbed her head, waved her arms, trembled to the screech of the guitar. She didn't care how crazy she looked. When another song came on, she played an air guitar, she screamed until she thought she'd burst a blood vessel in her neck, she got her rage out. She got her pain out. The songs helped her to do something with them.

Then when the song ended, she rested her head on the steering wheel before she lifted her head and looked at the structure in the distance. She didn't want to go back inside the house.

This big beautiful house filled with beautiful people and their rich people troubles.

She needed to get away. She'd hardly slept the night before, tossing in her bed hoping she was in the middle of a nightmare from which she could wake up. Yes, she had to get away. Away from the Fortunes. Away from Ava. Away from the memory of her greatest humiliation. Max's words swirled in her mind. *I never have nor will I ever be engaged to this woman. I may be single but do I look desperate?* The bastard treated her like pond scum. How could one little lie make a man so furious? The way he'd responded to her tiny fib one would have thought it was personal. But she didn't know him and he didn't know her. He was just a mean, rich bastard who took pleasure in stomping on those less powerful than him. How James could be friends with such a person was beyond imagination.

She drove back to her apartment and thought of never going back until she remembered she owed Rudy and James trusted her. She lay on her bed but couldn't quiet her thoughts or her grumbling stomach.

Several minutes later Desiree sat in a local gastro bar, the Fortunes would never even have heard of. The place was loud, with hamburgers the size of an ogre's fist, and orange vinyl seats. She was the only person who sat alone surrounded by food laden tables and boisterous late lunch crowds, but didn't care. She was used to being alone, as much as she didn't like it. But at least she was among her people. Those who had a car that sometimes didn't start, who had to budget a thousand dollar splurge (hell, let's be honest, a four hundred dollar splurge), who would never be featured in top news stories or have a senator and her family over for dinner.

"You look like somebody who needs a drink."

Desiree looked up from her cheese fries and saw a fresh faced black woman holding two pints of beer. The woman looked to be in her early-thirties, with wavy black hair and an engaging face that made Desiree think of spring time fairs and hot air balloon rides at dusk. Someone fun. She smiled. Company would be nice. Especially from someone with such a warm expression. It felt good to be liked again, even by a stranger. "Probably more than one."

The woman set the extra pint down in front of her. "That bad? Man trouble?"

"In a way."

"I've been there," she said with a laugh. "Now I'm older and hopefully a little wiser. Tell me your story and let me see if I can help you." She held out her hand. "Rachelle Weaver."

"Desiree Foster." She took a long swallow of her drink, the cold liquid quenching a thirst she didn't know she had, then said, "I don't think anyone could help me with this." She shook her head. "Maximillian Duchamp is in a category of his own."

"Max...Duchamp?"

It was the way Rachelle said his name that caught her interest. "Yes, do you know him?"

She flashed a sour grin. "Nearly married him."

"You're kidding." Why would a woman like her be in a place like this? Let alone be talking to someone like her?

Rachelle shook her head. "I wouldn't kid about something like that."

"I can't even imagine a sane woman dating him let alone...I'm sorry that came out wrong."

She laughed. "No, that's okay."

"Were you under hypnosis or something? Did your family need money for a surgery and he promised to—"

Rachelle laughed again. "No, nothing like that. He has his moments and can be charming when he wants to. I fell for the prospect of breaking past that wall he keeps around him. I failed. Most women do. It's a tempting, sexy challenge, but you end up losing your heart in the end. How did you get tangled up with him?"

"It was a stupid mistake. A total accident. I thought I'd made him up...anyway, the short of it is, he got upset about a tiny little lie I said about us and instead of handling it like a gentleman he completely blew it out of proportion."

"That's Max. He hates liars. You'd think he was a walking saint."

"I know. Judge and jury. That's him. Won't even listen to reason. I had a good one too."

"I'm sure you did, but that doesn't matter with a man with such rigid rules."

Desiree groaned. "To think he's actually friends with the Fortunes."

Rachelle gave a low whistle. "You know the Fortunes?"

"Sort of. I work for them. I help the youngest at the local community college."

"How well do you know them?"

"I just met them so, again, not much. They seem okay. I like James and Rudy. Jackson more than Ava and I won't even try to classify Edgar."

"From my understanding people like the Fortunes don't have friends as much as 'connections.' Max would be one. They serve each other."

"Figures. It's a world beyond me."

"I grew up on the peripherals of that world. My mother worked for the Duchamps. Max and I were friends at first as children. You wouldn't believe how small he was as a boy and so kind. I didn't really think much about him until he came back from university. Then I fell for him. He was so...amazing."

Desiree patted her hand in pity. "I suppose love is blind."

"Youth is too. He was everything that could make a young girl's heart skip a beat. I told him I loved him and he smiled. We dated, even though his father was against it. I think part of him used me to get back at his father, but I didn't know it at the time. Anyway, he proposed and I was overjoyed. I was willing to spend my life with him, but then I did one little thing wrong and he humiliated me. Cancelled the engagement and locked me out of his life. I'm still recovering."

Desiree frowned. "Yes, that sounds *exactly* like him. Be glad you escaped him. I'm sure being married to him would have been much worse."

"It's not something I share with people often, but I feel like I can trust you. That you'd understand. Most people wouldn't believe me."

"Why not?"

"They can't afford to. It's easier to side with a man like that." Rachelle lowered her voice. "And if you think he's bad, his sister is even worse. Beautiful and spoiled. Cold. I've known her since she was toddler and now she won't even look at me."

"You're better off without them both."

"This was fun. Want to do it again?"

"I'd love to." They exchanged contact information then Desiree left. She walked to her car with a new spring in her step, unbothered by the needles of rain splattering the parking lot.

Rachelle Weaver was exactly what she needed. A breath of fresh air from these cool sophisticates; these intellectual marvels. She was beautiful without being showy, refined without feeling off-limits. She had a ready smile, a pleasing demeanor. Everything Desiree dreamed of being. She wasn't off-putting like Ava. She was so relatable. And best of all she liked her.

She may have a new sister, but a new friend was just what she needed.

oney definitely had its privileges. The Fortunes' Bethany Beach house on the Delaware coast said it all.

At first Desiree was going to decline James's invite to go to the beach house the upcoming weekend, but when he hinted at a chance to reconnect with Rudy, plus the promise of a beach breeze and good seafood, she jumped at the chance.

Rachelle had helped her pack, since Desiree didn't want to stand out among the other beachgoers and Rachelle knew how to mingle with others in the exclusive zip code. They'd briefly gone shopping at a quirky thrift store Desiree liked to frequent and Rachelle helped her find outfits she never would have tried before.

"You'll be fine," she'd assured her as she went through Desiree's closet to complement some of the new outfits she'd bought. "Most of your clothes are serviceable."

Which was a far cry from the praise she'd hoped for. She may not win any fashion prizes, but she'd always thought she'd dressed well. Before she could say anything the doorbell rang. She opened the door and saw Laurence.

"Since you won't respond to my texts or calls I thought I'd come by," he said.

"I've been busy. What—" She stopped when his gaze shifted away from her to stare at something behind her.

She turned to see what had caught his attention and saw Rachelle sporting Desiree's yellow sunhat. "Oh, she's my new friend. She's saved me from going crazy. Rachelle, meet my brother Laurence. Laurence, Rachelle."

"A pleasure," she said shaking his hand.

Desiree half-expected him to bow and kiss it. Instead he flashed one of his awkward smiles. He was always a little shy with women. "Same."

"I'm going to the Fortune's beach house and Rachelle's helping me pack."

"You still could have phoned."

"I don't have much to report yet."

"Report?" Rachelle said with a sly grin. "Are you a spy?"

"No, it's...we might be related to the Fortunes by marriage. It's complicated."

"Do they know this?"

"They do now, but no one else knows."

"Mum's the word, darling." Rachelle mimed zipping her lips. "I know these rich people like to keep their secrets. Especially when it comes to bedroom antics. Which one of you is the love child?"

"It's not like that," Laurence said. "Ava—"

"And the Fortunes want us to keep their privacy," Desiree interrupted. While she could understand her new friend's curiosity she didn't want any gossip to get out. Ava was not someone she wanted to cross. "Could you give us a minute?" She waited for Rachelle to disappear back in her bedroom before she pulled her brother to the side and said in a low voice, "I didn't call because I had to tell Ava everything after this guy publicly humiliated me."

"She knows?"

"Don't worry, she won't contact Mom yet. We have time."

"Why did that guy—"

"It's a long story I want to forget. I only wanted you to know why I didn't call you. James is going to get a DNA test done and we should get the results in a couple weeks. I'll contact you then. He said he'll arrange everything."

"What's she like?"

"You'll find out soon enough. Now go and let me finish packing." She went back into her bedroom where her suitcase sat closed on the bed.

Rachelle spread her arms with a flourish. "Tada! You're all packed. Have a good time." She handed her the suitcase. "Your brother's cute. Is he single?"

"Very."

"I could change that."

"I doubt it. He's got another focus right now." She thought about telling her about his FIRE plan then changed her mind. If she stayed around him long enough, he'd share that himself. It was something he was proud of.

"I like a challenge."

She doubted Rachelle would last long with him. Most women got bored of Laurence quickly. Perhaps a date or two would be good for him even though she didn't expect their relationship to go anywhere. She didn't like him being so single-focused. "He loves buffalo wings and beer." She didn't add because they were cheap.

Rachelle winked. "Thanks for the tip. And here's my tip for you. Flaunt what you've got. You've got great eyes and legs. Work it."

Desiree felt her face warm. No one had ever told her that before. Rachelle not only made her feel good, she gave her confidence. "Thanks."

However, when she arrived at the beach house, she hesitated to wear the green and orange sarong she'd packed, when she saw Ava step out onto the pool deck in a black wrap dress that complemented her elegant figure. But when Toyin admired the color she was wearing and Jackson sent her a playful wink she decided to stop worrying about not measuring up and enjoy herself.

After a fun cram session with Rudy, who had a couple weeks left before the end of his course, he left her to go with James and Ava into town so she decided to walk barefoot along the beach. She drank in the ocean air and let the wet sand slide between her toes. She wished she'd been able to invite Rachelle to come with her. It would have been nice to have company she could easily relate to. Rudy was sweet, James was considerate, Jackson a flirt, Toyin kind and Ava...Ava was Ava, but they weren't her friends and it had grown awkward being around them. She wanted them to like her, and while she sensed that they did, her lie had damaged their complete trust in her and she knew she would have to work hard to get it back. She'd walked several yards past people strolling along the water's edge (a couple with two children, a young woman, two teenagers) when she heard someone shout.

She turned and saw a slender young woman in a violet sundress waving at her. The sun kept her from seeing the woman's face clearly.

"I thought it was you!" the young woman said then started running towards her. Desiree looked behind her to see if the woman was talking to someone else, but there was no one. She turned and as the woman got closer she saw her face and it all came rushing back.

"Felice!"

The woman hugged her and cried in delight, "I can't believe this. I thought I'd never see you again. I was so mad at myself for not getting your name and number. This is incredible. You look the same."

"You look amazing." And she did. Felice looked nothing like the pitiful woman who'd wanted her life to end five years ago. She looked healthy, vibrant and beautiful.

"It took a lot of reconstructive surgeries, but I'm nearly completely back to me."

"I'm so glad."

"When I woke up and saw the notes you'd taped together from my brother, on my bed, I cried. I also gave him the letter you wrote."

Desiree felt her face burn. She was slightly thrilled and also a little horrified at the same time. For all these years, Million had become almost a fantasy to her, she'd almost forgotten that the basis of him had been a real person. "Oh."

"He didn't say anything, he never says anything, but I knew he was touched. Your letter was so beautiful. I knew it was just what he needed." She looped her arm through Desiree's. "Are you here with anybody special?"

"Not really."

"Great. You have to come back to the beach house with me. I'll treat you to lunch and I'll tell you all that I've been up to and you'll do the same. And you'll have to spend a night or two. Lunch won't be enough."

Desiree smiled, Felice sounded like a woman used to getting her way. "That sounds like fun. I just have to talk to the people I'm staying with first."

"I'm sure they won't mind." She took Desiree's cell phone and put in the address. "Can you come by in an hour? I'll have to tell the chef."

"Uh...sure."

"Great! See you soon!"

When she told James about her plans he seemed pleased. They sat on the porch where bright sunlight and a cool sea breeze fought for attention among wicker furniture. "Rudy will miss you."

"If you don't think—"

"This break wasn't only for him. I'm glad you've found someone who's brought back your smile."

Desiree lowered her gaze, embarrassed that he'd noticed and had cared. He was such a kind man. "Thanks." She handed him a piece of paper. "Here's the address. I'll be back in two days."

James frowned at the address. "You're staying here?"

"Yes."

"She's a friend of Max's?"

Desiree shuddered in disgust. "I certainly hope not. Why?"

James tucked the note in his trouser pocket and shook his head. "No reason. Have fun."

She intended to. After a fun shopping spree with Rachelle only a day ago she looked forward to a sleepover with Felice. She wanted to know all about her and her mysterious brother.

"I met you at the most exciting time," Felice said as she and Desiree sat in the open living-dining-kitchen space finishing up a lunch of yellow rice and grilled flounder. Desiree was still trying to get over the extraordinary surroundings. Felice's beach house made the Fortune's look like a cottage. "My brother is determined to save his friends from a possible schemer."

"Schemer?"

"Yes, don't worry. We're used to them—gold diggers, opportunists, the like. My brother prides himself in rooting them out like an exterminator and keeping us all safe. He said this last one was really good and convincing but he's going to keep his eye on her.

"He's afraid for his friend so he even had this

woman's mother and brother followed and he may be onto something." She lowered her voice. "He thinks the brother is hiding something. He has a job where he makes decent money but lives in a tiny apartment in a cheap part of town. Where's the money going? Max is determined to find out and then let his friend know. He can be a protector that way."

"Oh." This was the Million she remembered Felice telling her about.

"Married?"

"No, I told you. After..." She bit her lip. "I don't think he ever will. But at least this new woman will keep him busy, I was afraid he'd only focus on work and," she rolled her eyes, "growing the empire. That's what Dad wants for him."

"I see. But he doesn't want that?"

"He has another business that's really his passion, not that he'd admit it."

"What about you Felice?

"I have a confession to make," she said looking suddenly guilty.

"What?"

"My name isn't Felice. I was in the hospital under a false name."

"Oh, that's okay."

"My real name is Gisele Duchamp."

"Duchamp?" Desiree said with a groan. "That's unfortunate. I recently met this awful man named—"

The sound of the front door closing caused Gisele to jump up. "That's my brother. We came up here together, but he went to do something in town. I texted him that you were here and I wanted him to meet you before he dashes off somewhere again. You're going to love him."

Anticipation knotted inside of her. After all these years she'd finally get to meet him. Desiree put on a bright smile and turned.

And nearly lost her lunch.

CHAPTER 26

*M*ax.

Max stood there. He stood there as if he belonged. The beast. The assassin. The cause of her greatest humiliation stood there and...wait...the assassin had a *sister*? A sister!!!

A sister who'd been in the hospital five years ago? No, something was wrong. The assassin couldn't have been the one who'd put flowers around Gisele's room and tucked in the special notes. He couldn't be the one who Felice/Gisele had told her about. The one she'd written the letter to. The one she'd been secretly dreaming about and writing to all these years. No, there had to be a mistake.

Max. Maximillian. Million. It all must be a strange coincidence or a terrible nightmare.

Gisele stood behind Desiree, resting her hands on Desiree's arms like she was a prize she'd won. "Here she is, Million. The one whose name I never got. I always felt so bad about it. Anyway, she's the one I told you about, who saved my life."

"I didn't do anything," Desiree said in a weak voice, "and now I think I should—"

"She's the one who tied your notes together," Gisele continued.

Please don't mention the letter. Please. Please. Please.

"And she wrote you that letter."

Let me just die now.

She wouldn't panic. She wouldn't run out of the room screaming. It wasn't a big deal. Maybe he never read it. He probably threw it away the moment he got it. Shredded it. Burned it. It was so silly and senti-mental a man like him wouldn't relate. He'd have no use for it.

She felt like such a fool. Her 'Million' had never existed. She'd created a false image of him in her mind. This man wasn't a person who felt pain, he caused it. He didn't need a friend. He didn't need anybody. Perhaps he wouldn't make the connection. She hadn't signed her name. Perhaps he'd forgotten his sister had even given him anything. Pleaseeee.... She hoped that was true. She would hate to have revealed anything important to a man like him. Perhaps he'd say: What letter? and his sister would be annoyed with him for forgetting and then they'd change the subject and...

However, there was something about his expression. Something she'd not expected to see. His face hadn't changed, but there was something about his eyes. His eyes gave him away. He remembered. How could he remember? That meant he'd read the letter? Him? This awful man had read her heartfelt words and remembered them?

The brief look came then went. He nodded his head. "Thanks for what you did."

"You're welcome."

Gisele rolled her eyes. "You're always so formal. At least kiss her on the cheek."

Desiree spun to her alarmed. "What?"

She turned her back to face him. "That's what he said he would do. He said if he ever met the woman who made his little sister happy, he'd kiss her on the cheek."

Max shook his head. "You said that, not me."

"Well, it's not a bad idea. Come on."

Desiree waved her hands frantic. "That's really not necessary."

"It's fine," Max said and kissed her on the cheek. For a man so cold, his lips felt hot, burning. He whispered, "Meet me in three hours, I'll send you the address," before he straightened and looked at his sister. "I have to go."

She pulled a face. "You only just got back."

"I'll see you later." He left the room.

Gisele sighed. "Isn't he the greatest? He's shy. But I already told you that."

"Right," Desiree said. But now she realized all that Gisele had told her had to be a lie.

His heart wouldn't stop racing. He'd come to the beach house to reassess the woman who had upset his plans at the Fortune house and here she was. He marched into his bedroom and closed the door, searching his mind for what to do next. He always knew what to do, but this time his mind was blank. All it could repeat was: Her. It was her. The One. *She* was The One.

Max took a well-preserved piece of paper out of his wallet. He'd carried the letter she had written to him every day since he'd received it, as a reminder that he wasn't alone. That there was someone else out there who understood.

Desiree? Her? She was the one?

I'll admit to being half in love with you. He'd remembered every word.

She was nothing like he'd pictured. The woman who'd written the letter was more...sophisticated. More like him. He'd never imagine a woman who'd held a series of jobs and didn't have a university degree. And yet...she was also exactly as he'd imagined her to be. Charming, considerate. Those were the traits James had seen and he'd been completely blind to. Now pieces of the puzzle came together. Desiree had been genuine. She was someone special. Someone kind enough to gain his sister's trust and make her happy. Five years ago he'd feared he'd lose her forever.

But Desiree had saved her life and that had bonded her to him in his heart. A place he kept locked.

He'd been annoyed with himself for how attracted he'd initially been to her when she'd stood in the great room and revealed why she was at the Fortune house. Noticing anything about her, like her full lips, curvy figure and pretty eyes, made him feel like a traitor to logic. He'd fallen for a smile before and false sincerity. Now he knew his feelings for her had all been real.

He inwardly groaned as more pieces of the puzzle came together. Now everything made sense. This was how she'd known everything about him. She wasn't a devious schemer. She'd made up a story to impress Rudy by using what his sister had told her. He was strangely touched that she remembered every detail. She was genuine. Sincere. He couldn't believe someone like that actually existed. At least he now knew his friend wasn't in trouble. James's instincts had been right, she wasn't a threat. He'd miscalculated and now he had to make it up to her.

If he told her how he felt, maybe they could stop pretending. Maybe he could sleep again. He hadn't been able to since he'd met her. Since he'd been forced to apologize.

He told himself he thought of her because of how much she reminded him of his ex. Why else would he continue to investigate her mother and brother? He hated liars. But he knew he was also lying to himself. He still remembered the soft tone of her voice as she spoke to Rudy, the blanket admiration in her gaze when she looked at James, the bright smile on her face as she talked to Jackson, while Max studied her from the balcony.

Telling her what her letter had meant to him probably wouldn't lead to anything, but that wasn't the point. The point was to regain his sanity. To get his thinking back on track. He'd been distracted too much lately and she was the cause. He could no longer deny it. Part of him didn't want to. She was the woman who'd written the letter that had kept him company during some of his darkest times. She'd made his sister see joy in life again, she'd shown him another way of looking at the world. It wasn't his fault he'd fallen a little under her spell. How could he help it? She was fresh air. He felt he could breathe again.

Until her letter, he hadn't realized he'd stopped. He hadn't realized when he'd stop feeling human. When everything around him was rote and grey.

She changed that.

But he now regretted what had happened at the party. He'd been overzealous. His past had made him hard. Now that he'd found her he didn't want to lose her, again. He knew it would take some persuasion but the fact that she was here, that she remembered so much would work in his favor. He'd do something, anything, to make her forgive him.

Something special. As special as her.

He pulled out his cell phone and called his assistant and told him what he wanted.

Holland delicately cleared his throat. "It's rather short notice."

"I know it's short notice," Max snapped. "I still want it done." It had to be done.

And it was. Three hours later he walked into a private booth at the Taylor's Seaside restaurant surrounded by the hazy glow of candles and the scent of roses. Over to the side on a small side table, he had a covered box of chocolates. When he gave it to her she would see inside that the chocolates spelled: Forgive Me.

He sat down at the table and waited. He half feared she wouldn't show up.

But she did.

Desiree entered the room wearing a lovely green dress (his favorite color. Did she know that?) and his worry ebbed. Now he could admit to himself that he thought she was beautiful. That he wanted to know her better. He had a chance. A second chance to make things right.

CHAPTER 27

He watched her take a seat.

"Thanks for coming."

"What's all this about?"

Max took a deep breath. "I wanted to apologize. I was wrong to treat you the way I did. You're not one of the typical parasites my sister picks up. I'd like a chance to get to know you better. Maybe be friends. Go out for a drink." He reached for his wallet. "That letter—"

"Stop."

He blinked. "What?"

"I didn't tell your sister anything and I don't plan to." She shot a glance at his wallet. "Do you think that by flashing your money your flimsy apology will change anything? Do you want to make sure that the schemer in your midst will go away for the right price?"

"No, you don't—"

"Your sister really doesn't know anything about you, does she? That letter was a mistake. I realize that now. I'd sooner write a love letter to Mussolini than draft two lines to you. If I'd known you'd receive that letter, I wouldn't have written a single word."

Her words penetrated deep. Pierced his soul. He could take any other insult. He could take her despising what he did, what he looked like, his wealth. He was used to that. But to despise him as a man. As a person. Especially when he couldn't share, couldn't tell anyone, how much that letter had meant to him. How much he'd re-read it. How he knew it by heart. How it made him feel less alone in this world. And now, he no longer had that. She was telling him it was a mistake. That every word meant for him was a lie. He wanted her to stop talking, he wished he'd stopped her before she said the words, but now that they were spoken they shattered every pleasant memory of the letter he'd once had.

"You're cold, arrogant, pathetic—"

He shook his head, feeling his temper rise. "I understand that what I did was wrong. But I had my reasons. To take one action and think you can do this character assassination—"

"One act?" Desiree's voice cracked in surprise. "I have more than enough proof to know your true character. Not only did you humiliate me, you had my mother and brother followed? Like criminals?"

"I wanted to find out more about your story. The Fortunes might dig deep, but I always dig deeper. I didn't approach them. I was simply gathering information."

"I don't care! You not only treated me like a criminal, treated my family like conspirators but you also hurt a friend of mine in the most cruel way."

"Friend?"

"Rachelle Weaver. She told me all that you did to her. You humiliated her just as you did me. Publicly and cruelly. Just because of one little lie."

"A little lie?" He laughed without humor. "Is that what she called it?"

"I'm sure to you any kind of misrepresentation is tantamount to being a traitor."

"Did you even consider there are two sides to the story?"

"Oh, I pretty much know your side. You're at least consistent. Be patient. Wait for the best opportunity so that the most damage can be done and then attack. Does that sound about right?"

He rubbed his forehead. "I had my reasons."

"Of course, and your reasons matter more than anyone's pride or dignity. You're the only one who is right and justified. I can't believe you'd think that I would want anything from you." She swept her hand indicating their elegant surroundings. "That this blatant, vulgar show of all your money would impress me. Just because I don't have a lot of money, doesn't make me desperate. I could be starving and I wouldn't be desperate enough to even eat a slice of bread with a man like you or—"

Max held up his hand. He cleared his throat before he spoke afraid his voice would shake. "You've made your point. I'm sorry I wasted your time." He stood. "If you need anything just let them know. Excuse me." He nodded and left.

He had to get away.

He had to get away from her, from the pain the sight of her caused him.

But he couldn't run away from her words. They echoed in his mind. *If I'd known you'd receive that letter, I wouldn't have written a single word.* His heart cracked. His throat closed. As he walked to his car, he took the letter out of his wallet. He should tear it up. Burn it. To think he'd been about to reveal all she'd meant to him these years. She'd not only saved his sister's life, but his own.

He still remembered entering his sister's hospital room with a feeling of dread and seeing a string of his words laid out on her bed and Gisele smiling.

Someone had gotten her to smile. He couldn't believe it. She hadn't smiled like that since she was a small child.

"Did you see her?" she asked him.

"See who?"

"Oh, I'm so stupid. I didn't ask her name. She came in and talked to me and did this and...oh Million she was wonderful."

He sat beside her bed and gently covered her hand. "Are you sure you weren't dreaming?"

"It felt like a dream. But then she left this." She handed him the letter.

He frowned seeing that it had been hastily refolded. "You read it."

"Of course I read it."

He tucked it away in his trouser pocket. "I'll read it later."

And he did. Much later. Nearly a week. He'd remembered the letter when he'd been cleaning out his pockets to get his trousers dry cleaned and saw it again. He'd read it that night in his room. No one had written to him before. Let alone someone he'd never met. He'd read it with a sense of wariness. What did this strange woman have to say? Would she blame him for what had happened to his sister? He was used to blame. But her first words, the first line, had been like a healing balm to his soul. *I'll admit to being half in love with you.*

Someone was on his side. Someone didn't see him as the enemy. Someone understood his guilt, how he felt he'd failed his sister. Then she'd signed the note 'A friend' and he loved her for it. He loved her because few people had wanted to be his friend without an agenda and this offer of friendship had been given freely, generously, purely.

He'd imagined her as some kindly older woman who saw him as a son. But when he asked Gisele for a description the image changed.

But he never pictured her as Desiree.

He could never have imagined a woman like Desiree. Pretty, selfless, caring.

Desiree. The one woman who hated him. He looked at the letter and gripped it in his fist. He had to get rid of it. Its magic had been lost. He had to throw it away. He crumpled it up into a ball and marched down to the beach. He'd throw it in the ocean. Let the water wash the words away.

But when he reached the beach, he couldn't throw it. He looked up at the dark sky pocketed with stars and listened to the sound of the waves crawling up the sand. Hope lingered. Hope that he wasn't a monster, that he could be human again despite what Rachelle had turned him into. The letter was still his lifeline even if it hadn't been meant for him.

Rachelle. She'd won again. How could she still destroy everything that surrounded him?

What a fool he was to think that somewhere out there someone else understood him.

He could hear his father's laughter, reminding him again of how stupid he was. He saw the gaping black hole of the monster house where his grandfather had lived and wondered if that still could be his fate.

Max sat down on the soft sand and smoothed out the letter. He folded it and tucked it away. He didn't need to destroy it. He'd just never look at it again. He'd keep it as a reminder for how foolish he'd been. He'd been weak. A weakness he'd never share, and never succumb to again. He'd stay on his guard. Strength came from control. Rachelle had taught him that. A hard won lesson he'd never forget.

CHAPTER 28

*A*hhhh!

If only she had her car! Why hadn't she driven up to Bethany Beach in her car? She had nowhere to blast her music and scream. Oh God how she wanted to scream!

Desiree paced the spacious guest room of the Duchamp beach house, past the large sleigh bed and white linen door chest, still trembling with anger. Who did Max think he was?

Friends? Drinks? Was he out of his mind? Did he think she was so desperate that she'd take his kind of abuse? He clearly thought she'd be grateful. A man like him would. He would think that any action he did would be forgiven. But she'd never forgive him. Ever. Rachelle had shown her his true character. His true way of being. At least she wasn't heartbroken, even though it did burn that she'd been deceived by Gisele and persuaded to write to someone who wasn't real. Gisele didn't know who her brother really was.

How humiliating! To think she'd bared her heart to someone like that. To someone so...awful. So arrogant. Desiree squeezed her eyes shut and bit her knuckles. If she couldn't blast her music, she could pour her heart out to Million.

She reached for her cell phone then stopped. No Million was dead. Max had killed him. She had no outlet now. She punched her pillow. Dammit! She was all alone again.

It was a good lesson. Like her mother, there were people she couldn't please; unlike her mother, there were people who weren't worth the effort. Why did he have to mention the letter at the restaurant? It could have been something avoided, ignored.

But she couldn't get his sister's description of him out of her thoughts. He'd seemed so ordinary then. Relatable. Gisele didn't know her brother very well. Desiree couldn't understand why Gisele would ever worry about him. What manipulative tactic had he used to convince his sister otherwise? It was all so terrible. But now it was over.

Max seemed briefly, genuinely, startled by her words. She was glad. She liked shaking him up a bit. He didn't like her before; he'd like her even less now.

But she still felt a loss. The loss of the man she thought she'd written the letter to. For. What a waste.

Her brother was quiet. Too quiet. She could feel him pulling in on himself. Gisele had snuck down that night for a snack and found him sitting alone in the living room with only the light from the TV illuminating his face. He usually loved coming to the beach house, it gave them both a sense of calm. But there was something different about him. Something had changed since this afternoon. She walked into the living room and turned on the light. He turned to her. The mask he used to protect himself was clear in his guarded expression. That was never a good sign. He'd only done that after...but maybe she was being too sensitive. Things were looking up for them now. She'd finally met her guardian angel again. So many things felt possible.

"Can't sleep?"

"Hmm."

She sat down beside him and nudged him with her elbow. "Where did you disappear to? First you left and then Desiree told me she had a quick errand she had to run for the Fortunes. When she came back she said she was too tired to talk and went straight to her room. Do you think she's okay?"

He turned back to the flat screen. "I wouldn't know."

"Are you worried about something?"

He shook his head.

"You're quiet. More quiet than usual. Is something wrong?"

He shook his head again.

"Isn't Desiree great? I'm *so* glad you got to meet her."

"Hmm."

"But you should stop doing that."

"Doing what?"

"Scaring her. When she first saw you she looked like she was about to faint." Gisele giggled with amusement.

She saw him tense. "I scare people, it's what I do. What do you want?"

"You don't have to be scary."

"It's my face. I can't help it."

"If you smiled more—"

He rubbed his chin irritated. "It wouldn't help."

"If you hadn't scurried away like a shy kid you could have talked to her more. I'll invite her—"

"No, don't do that. She's your friend. She'd want to spend time with you. Not me."

She looped her arm through his. "You don't know—"

"I do know."

She sighed feeling the tension in him. "Don't let Rachelle—"

"Rachelle won," he said in a soft voice. "I can't beat her."

"What?"

"Never mind."

She stroked his arm, sad she'd upset him. "I'm sorry I brought her up. I know we both promised never to mention her again. She didn't win, we both survived and that's because of you."

"Get your snack and go back to bed."

"No."

He sighed. "What do you want?"

She wanted to see him happy. She wanted to see him look less miserable. Something was troubling him, but he wasn't in the mood to share and she wouldn't force him.

However, she knew one way to distract him. "There's this guy."

He turned sharply to her. "No."

"You didn't even let me finish.'

"Because I don't want to hear it. Any time you start a sentence with 'There's this guy' it doesn't end well."

"Not all the time."

"I said no. I'm not giving one of your new loves a job."

"Even if he's great?"

"If he's great, he can find his own job."

Gisele playfully rolled her eyes. "You act as if you want me to stay single forever like you."

"You won't be, so that doesn't bother me."

She paused for a moment then quietly asked, "What bothers you?"

He turned his attention back to the TV screen. "Goodnight, Gisele."

Gisele got up and turned off the lights, cloaking him in darkness except for the glare of the TV. She then glanced back at him, her heart heavy. He was so alone; she knew that Desiree could be the key to healing his hurt. A hurt he wouldn't share with anyone. Perhaps if given a chance, Desiree could help him.

PATHETIC, *cruel, disgusting, vulgar.*

Desiree's accusations continued to whirl in his mind as he stared at the screen.

Him. Max Duchamp. A man who prided himself on being a good friend, a good son, a good brother. A man of integrity, dignity. He didn't suffer fools gladly, he could be ruthless. He could be cold. But pathetic? Never. Cruel? Only to his enemies.

And Rachelle Weaver was enemy number one.

He had to vindicate himself against her lies. She was the liar who had turned his life upside down. Who'd helped him hone his skill to weed others out.

He turned off the TV, went to his room and sat at his desk.

He couldn't let another day pass with Rachelle's lies as the only thing Desiree knew about him. Desiree may not like him for other reasons but not based on Rachelle's words. He'd have his say.

He opened a drawer and pulled out several sheets of paper and a pen. She'd given him a letter once. Now it was his turn.

CHAPTER 29

It was a cool morning when the assassin arrived. Desiree sat on the porch looking out at the ocean. She'd woken up before Gisele and was enjoying the promise of a new day when Max arrived and held out a letter to her.

"Please read this then burn it."

She glanced at it with little interest then shifted her gaze to the ocean. "Maybe I should just burn it first and save us both time."

He sighed. "I don't ask favors easily, but I'm asking this." He continued to hold the letter out to her.

She snatched it from him. "Okay."

"Thanks," he said before he left.

Desiree unfolded the letter surprised by its length. She looked at his bold strokes and upright handwriting. She felt like tossing it into the ocean, but she had said she would read it and the thought of burning it afterwards gave her a perverse pleasure even if she would be doing it because of his instructions.

Desiree,

I'm writing this letter more for my sister's sake than for my own. Although you might think I'm a complete heartless egoist I won't stand by and let you accuse me of manipulating my sister. She is the most important person to me and having you thinking her too stupid to realize the true nature of her brother, or naïve, that I'm such a clever manipulator that she doesn't know the truth, are two lies that I will not let stand unchecked.

Desiree rolled her eyes. Of course you won't. You're the liar hunter. Jerk.

I'm not a man of many words, but I have a few misunderstandings I want to clear up between us.

Misunderstandings? That's what he called them? Typical arrogance.

First, I already apologized for the event at the Fortune house. I thought I made my reasons clear. I believed you were a threat to my friends. They've been threatened before. People in our position cannot be too welcoming to strangers. I admit that I handled the matter badly and both you and James showed me the error of my ways. If you want to continue to hold a grudge so be it. But just as you didn't take me at my word, I also was still hesitant about you.

Yes, I did look into your family's background and thought your brother's living arrangements worrying. Why would a young man with a decent income live like that? Was his money going to a particular vice that you were supporting? What secrets were you hiding? I couldn't find anything, and thought perhaps he's just incredibly frugal and left it at that.

Your parents were equally troubling. I knew about your mother's many hospitalization and a lesser person could be persuaded to seize an opportunity to milk a possible rich relation. I see now that my suspicions were incorrect but my concerns were not unfounded.

Desiree shook her head. There he goes again making himself look good. Unfounded. Who uses words like that anymore?

And now I will talk about your friend Rachelle Weaver. What I am about to tell you must remain between us. You must never reveal a word I say, and I ask that you burn this letter until every inch of it is ash.

With pleasure.

Rachelle Weaver was the daughter of our house manager.

What the hell was a house manager?

A wonderful woman who helped make our house run efficiently. Rachelle and I grew up together and were friends. I had only a few friends back then. I grew to love her as did my sister. But then her mother got ill and had to leave us. I later got in contact with Rachelle to see how she was doing. And when I saw her again I loved her much more than I had in the past. She told me she wanted to go to school to study business, but didn't have the funds. I paid her way and her housing and everything she needed. We planned to marry after she graduated.

But the wedding wasn't to be. It was through an acquaintance of mine that I discovered that Rachelle hadn't gone to university. For the entire four years she'd been taking my money and traveling and living free with various 'friends'. I confronted her about this lie and she tearfully told me that she hadn't meant to fool me. That she'd been so overwhelmed the first year she'd taken a little break and then the break became longer until she felt that she couldn't catch up, but she didn't want to disappoint me so she'd kept up the façade.

I told her the wedding was over. That I couldn't marry her. We parted ways and I thought that was it. I let everyone believe she'd left me, for the sake of her pride and mine, and wanted nothing to do with her. I didn't let anyone else know the reason for our breakup and that was probably my worst mistake. Because a year later she reconnected with my sister.

I don't know how she did it, but my sister was young and impressionable at the time and still loved her like a sister and after a brutal breakup Rachelle convinced her that a breast enlargement would help Gisele build her confidence.

She made her keep this a secret from the family and flew with my sister to the butcher who nearly killed her. It was only when she collapsed at home and was rushed to the hospital that she finally admitted what she'd done.

Rachelle disappeared and we've never seen her again. I have no doubt that she hurt my sister to get back at me and she succeeded. My parents have yet to forgive me. Gisele now suffers from anxiety attacks.

Rachelle Weaver is a consummate actress. I don't blame you for falling for her charms. I fell for them myself. It is my greatest embarrassment. My greatest heartbreak. You came into my sister's life at the most crucial time. My *life too. You may regret every word you wrote to me. But I'll never regret reading them.*

And that's all I have to say.

M

Desiree stared at the letter.

She didn't know how to respond. She felt a renewed anger and sadness. On one hand Max still felt justified for suspecting her, he didn't find anything wrong with humiliating her or investigating her family. But now she knew the reason. If she'd been in his place, could she trust again after having been so betrayed?

Rachelle. *Her* Rachelle had stolen his money, betrayed his trust, lied to him, and used his sister for revenge?

Now that she thought about it, it was sort of strange how free Rachelle was with her information about Max but never gave her any particulars. How she let Desiree lead the conversation as if reading her. She was so angry at Max that she didn't question Rachelle about anything. What was the little lie that had so upset him? Why hadn't she thought to ask? She had been so eager to paint an ugly picture of him she'd welcomed any criticism she could find. That had made her an easy mark.

And Gisele had told her about a family friend who'd abandoned her. Rachelle had been clever enough not to mention that. Desiree sighed feeling ashamed of herself. She'd been vulnerable because of her anger at Ava and Max and fallen for false intimacy and fake smiles.

She'd let Rachelle into her confidence without any hesitation. She'd wondered how James could love a woman like Ava, but perhaps she wasn't as cold as she seemed.

Desiree folded up the letter. She still didn't like him, but she couldn't hate him as she once had. The letter made him too human.

He'd been in love.

He'd loved a woman who'd hurt him deeply. Who'd also hurt his little sister. She couldn't imagine how much that pain must linger. She'd hate anyone hurting Laurence.

Desiree sighed with regret. She could no longer think of him as an assassin. Just a flawed man with a painful past. When she burned his letter that evening, after a fun day with Gisele and rereading it once more, it didn't give her the pleasure she thought it would. She felt as if she were carrying a heavy secret. Not even his sister knew the reason for his broken engagement, that kind of trust was...rare and special.

Reminding her of the man who'd filled his sister's hospital room with flowers and wrote his love for her on tiny note cards.

A man she couldn't categorize as either enemy or friend.

CHAPTER 30

She wasn't supposed to dream about him.

She wasn't supposed to imagine Max's hard mouth, covering her own, softening hers with gentle persuasion. She wasn't supposed to think about the feel of his tongue, the feel of his hands sliding down her arms, his hard body pressed against hers. It was wrong in so many ways. She knew what he was. Who he was. She should imagine him looking over her body with judgment in his gaze, calculating every flaw, instead...instead she imagined his dark gaze heated with lust. Lust for every luscious curve (she imagined he liked curvy women), watched his Adams' apple move as he swallowed. He wanted her bad. Bad in every way and she let him have her because she wanted him too. She wanted to hear the hot whisper of his words "I don't regret a thing."

She was hot...so hot, and only grew hotter as his heavy body covered hers, every sensation springing to life.

"I know you want me," her dream Max said, while he slid his arms around her. "It wasn't a mistake that you mentioned my name. You could have chosen anyone, made up any name, but you chose me because if you were honest, you'd have to admit that the moment you saw me, there was something there."

"No."

"That letter wasn't a mistake either. Even though you didn't know it was me, you can't deny that the man described was someone you wanted to know. The man I am. Now you're afraid."

"I'm not afraid." She breathed the words wanting to feel angry, his voice remained in shadow above her even though she knew it was him, dreams were strange like that. Instead of anger, she felt fear and resentment, this dream-Max knew her too well. Knew her innermost desires. The ones she hadn't even realized yet.

"You can't hate me anymore. You never really did. It was embarrassment. But you sensed something when you saw me, didn't you? You wanted me to like you. You still do. Now that you know who I really am. You've waited for me. There has been no one else in your life, in your thoughts for, all these years except for me."

She was now wrapped in his arms, she should push him away, she should see this whole thing as a nightmare instead of one delicious dream. Desiree turned her head away, she didn't want to hear him speak, and he stopped talking. He let his mouth become occupied with her neck, then her stomach, then her...she should wake up now. This was something he'd never do. She wouldn't let him.

But she did. She did until she jolted awake, her body warm and wet. She pressed her legs closed. She'd change her panties later, she was still too shocked to move. To dream of him like that? To have thoughts do that to her? Why? How could one letter change her like this? How could she face him again?

It was all in her mind. It was anger finding a release in a strange way. That was all. It didn't mean anything.

Of course that rationale didn't help when she saw Max the following morning sitting at the breakfast table.

She briefly thought of leaving, but didn't want to do the cowardly thing. "Gisele is still in bed," she said just to fill the silence.

"She likes to sleep late."

She filled up her plate with the items laid out for breakfast. She chose a bagel with cream cheese and melon slices before she poured herself coffee. She sat down and realized too late she'd taken the seat opposite him.

He studied her. "Did you—"

"Yes, I burnt the letter." She bit into the bagel. She didn't want to talk. She didn't want to look at him. She wanted to eat then leave. Maybe he'd do her a favor and leave first.

"Did it upset you?"

She looked at him surprised, which was a mistake. First because she didn't want to look at him and remember her naughty thoughts and second, because his piercing eyes always made her feel like a suspect in an interrogation room. "Why would it upset me?"

He shrugged. "I don't know. You look terrible."

She sighed. "Can't the insults come after coffee?" She took another bite. He probably thought she was a pig, she didn't care.

"It's not an insult, it's an observation. Didn't you sleep well?"

Was he actually going to pretend to care? "Hardly. Thanks to you."

"Me?"

"Yes."

"So it was the letter."

"It wasn't the letter."

"Then what was it?"

Desiree set her bagel down, took a long swig of her coffee then sat back in her chair. "You don't want to know."

"Yes, I do."

It was those eyes that got her. Maybe he should know. Maybe she should shock—no disgust—him a little bit, then he'd leave her alone.

"I had a dream...or rather nightmare...about a man in my room. In my bed. It was a strange dream...I mean nightmare...filled with symbolism."

Max frowned. "What does that have to do with me?"

"You were the man." She picked up her bagel and took another bite to hide her grin.

"What was I doing there?"

"You really want to know?"

"No, I ask these questions so I can hear myself think."

"Sarcasm doesn't suit you."

"Neither does impatience. Why was I in your dream?"

Desiree looked at him again, this time surprised. The look of the interrogator was still there, but there was another expression too. Interest. Unadulterated interest. She'd intrigued him somehow. Was he such an egoist that he wanted to know everything she thought about him? Did he imagine her killing him in her dream? If he expected that, he was in for a surprise.

Perhaps if she told him the truth, he'd be so revolted and condescending that she'd hate him—fully, completely—and then never have him enter her dreams again. That would be a win. She needed that armor back. "All right. I'll tell you. But you can't tell anyone about this, okay?"

He nodded.

"It didn't start in my bedroom. It started in a forest. A dark forest and I was walking towards a light. I was wrapped only in a towel."

"Nothing underneath?"

"That's what wrapped only in a towel means."

"Just trying to make sure."

"Do you want to know the color and the fabric?"

"If you want."

He was being sarcastic, but she'd humor him. "A bright red plush terry fabric."

"Like Little Red Riding Hood."

"No, not like Little Red Riding Hood. You have a hard time just listening, don't you?"

Max shrugged. "I'm making a reference."

"Do you want me to continue or not?"

"Go on.

"I felt the presence of a man behind me."

"The Wolf."

Desiree made a low noise in her throat. "This is a dream not a fairytale. What is wrong with you?"

"You said it was a dream filled with symbolism. I was only trying to—"

"Be quiet. It wasn't the Wolf. It was a man. I was frightened, but he whispered 'Do not to be afraid'. It was a voice I'd heard before."

"And you knew it was mine?"

"I didn't say it was yours."

He leaned forward, resting his arms on the table. "There were two men in your dream?"

"Do you want me to finish this or not?"

"Can you blame me for being curious?"

She folded her arms.

"Okay, go on."

"The familiar voice assured me that I would be safe if I stayed along the path. And I wanted to but then the path disappeared and I didn't know where to go so I kept walking until the forest turned into my bedroom and suddenly I was wrapped up in silk sheets."

"The towel was gone?"

Desiree paused, surprised he was keeping track. "Yes, and now I was entangled in these sheets."

"Were they red too?"

What was it with him and the color? And something had changed about him. The interrogation gaze was gone, replaced by a mesmerizing gleam. He had this waiting, tense air about him. He licked his lip, she didn't know why. He'd already finished his food. Was it impatience? Irritation? "No, the sheets were more maroon."

"Hmm." It sounded like a strangled groan. But he didn't look bored so she continued.

"And there was the man again. He didn't let me see his face."

"But you knew it was me."

She sighed. Why was he so focused on himself being in her dream? He must already realize that she wasn't torturing him. "I didn't say it was you."

"But you said I was in your dream. How could I be in your dream if you never see my face?"

"You're right. Maybe I was wrong. Except...never mind." She lifted her bagel.

He grabbed her wrist before she brought it to her mouth, startling her. He quickly released her and sat back. "Sorry." He cleared his throat. "Except what?"

She looked at him. Finally really looked at him and was surprised that she had his full attention. He stared at her spellbound. No man had ever looked at her like that. It felt wonderful. Empowering. She had this arrogant man as her captive audience. She had to bite back a grin. She'd expected horror. Why would it matter to him if he was in her dream or not? That didn't matter, she'd milk the moment as much as she could.

"The man...he held me in his arms and whispered his name."

"My name."

"Yes, and he wanted me to say it."

His voice deepened. "And did you?"

"Yes."

He licked his lip again. "How?"

For some reason the way he licked his lip made her

feel hot and hungry. Desiree finished her bagel and chewed slowly before she swallowed. "How did I say his—your name?"

Max nodded, his eyes never leaving her face.

Desiree bit her lip. This was getting a little too real. She felt her heart pounding, her breathing shallow, this wasn't how this was supposed to go. "It doesn't matter."

"Yes, it does," Max said with such force that she jumped. "I want to picture it," he continued.

She licked her lip. Fine if he wanted to prolong this torture that was clearly bothering him she would continue. She leaned in closer, lowered her voice and whispered, "I said Max...Oh Max..." She paused and then when she spoke her words were merely a breath, "My dear Max." She sat back. "Like that." She reached for her coffee and took a long swallow.

"And what did I—uh he do?"

"He smiled and then he peeled the sheets away and..." She stopped. This was getting out of control.

"And?"

"I wake up."

Max blinked as though waking from his own dream. He frowned. "You're lying."

"I'm lying?" Her brows shot up. "You're calling me a liar again?"

Max quickly shook his head. "No. I'm not. But I don't believe you woke up. You just don't want to tell me the rest of your dream."

"Nightmare. It scared me. I was afraid."

His steady, dark gaze held her still. "Did I hurt you? Were you scared?"

She felt hotter than a furnace. She reached for her fork then set it down again when she saw her hand shaking. "Doesn't matter. Don't be so serious. I told you it was a dream."

"I thought you said it was a nightmare."

"It was a little bit of both."

"A dream when I wasn't there and then a nightmare afterwards?"

"Maybe."

His assistant entered the room. "Are you ready for—"

Max cut him off with a dismissive gesture. "I haven't finished yet."

The assistant looked at Max's empty plate. "But—"

"I need twenty minutes," he said through tight teeth.

The man nodded then left.

Desiree looked at Max suspicious.

He wasn't leaving. Was she the reason? Had she affected him so much that he couldn't stand? She didn't dare glance down to see if anything showed beneath the glass table. That was too much to believe.

She'd never seen his eyes so dark before, they shone with an intensity she'd never noticed. She wasn't sure if he was angry or aroused. She must be dreaming again, this man wouldn't care. He had been with better, seen better. He'd said so himself. *I may be single but do I look desperate?* Those words would never leave her. Maybe he was hiding his anger that he dare enter her dream without his permission. Perhaps he wanted to charge her a fee.

"Can I guess?" Max finally said in a husky whisper.

A whisper that should have frightened her, but seemed to draw her closer instead.

"Guess what?"

"What happened."

"I told you I woke up."

"Before you woke up. I...I mean this man who you thought was me...peeled away the sheets and touched you all over. He started with his hands on your hips even though he wanted to start elsewhere, but you wouldn't know this."

"No," she breathed unable to believe they were playing this dangerous game. He'd changed the rules on her.

"His arms are around you, he's covering your body, tasting you slowly. Soooo slowly. Starting with..." His eyes dipped to her chest. She could feel her nipples harden, but he didn't say a word. He didn't need to.

Desiree swallowed hard. "Not my throat?"

Max shook his head. "He'll get to that later."

"He likes to take his time?"

"He feels like he has plenty of it...but even then he won't waste a moment."

"I see."

Max bit his lower lip. "You taste so good. He can't get enough. And he starts to do things, lots of things, that leave you hot, wet, wanting."

"Like what?"

"Like—" Max stopped and looked away, a sly smile dancing on his lips. "Things that would give you nightmares for days. Maybe even weeks." His eyes met hers, his voice low. "Or maybe even years."

The way he drew out the word *years* made her skin tingle. For a moment she could pretend he was her Million, the fantasy man she'd dreamt about, longed for. "What kind of things? Give me a taste." She shook her head. "I mean a hint."

Max rested his chin in his hand. "That wouldn't be fair. I don't want to be another reason you can't sleep tonight. I wouldn't want you thinking about those things."

"But you said this is how my dream truly ended, how can I know if I have nothing to compare it to?"

"I think we both know we've taken this far enough."

"Afraid you'll have nightmares tonight?"

Max rubbed his forehead. "I think I'm in the middle of one right now."

He might as well have poured cold water over her. She pushed her chair back and stood up. "Of course, it would be that way to you."

He stared up at her surprised. "What's with the tone? You're no happier about this than I am."

"I didn't sound disgusted."

"I'm not...what I said came out wrong."

"You'd better not tell anyone."

"Who would I tell?" He pushed back his chair. "Do you really want to see what you've done to me?"

She held out her hand, refusing to look down at his trousers. "No."

"Then be careful how you play with me."

"I'll remember that." She marched out of the dining room.

Telling him about her dream hadn't gotten the

response she'd hoped. He was supposed to make her angry at him for being disgusted by it, instead she was still aroused. Aroused by someone like him. She'd let him mock her and...dammit seduce her. She now knew he would enter her thoughts again. What were the amazing things he could do to her body? She should have been repelled by the thought of his mouth anywhere near her body let alone covering her breasts. His tongue...nope. She was not going down that path. That was mere madness. First the letter and now this.

He was taunting her. Teasing her. Why had she liked it? Why wasn't she justifiably angry, outraged? Why had he made her say his name like that? Why had she?

Saying his name in a whisper made her see him, briefly, just briefly, as the sexy man in her dreams. The devastating sexy man who had taken over her body and mind and she'd enjoyed the surrender.

But she couldn't.

He was a bastard. That was how she had to think about him. To think about him in any other way was crazy and she'd been crazy enough to dream about him and then even hint about her dream about him and now...now she couldn't stop thinking about him without her face growing hot and she wanted—needed—to hate him as she had before. Remember how he humiliated her, how he'd insulted her. Had her family followed. He was a distrustful man. That was who he was. A cold hearted bastard with dark sexy eyes.

Nope, she'd forget about the sexy eyes part. She was here for his sister and then she'd go home. Her mother was reuniting with the daughter she truly loved and all was well with the world.

It didn't matter that she didn't have a real job. That she didn't have a relationship. That Ava already had it all. Gorgeous husband who adored her? Check! Fulfilling and satisfying career? Check! Great family relationship? Double check. Gorgeous looks to match the gorgeous house and husband? Check, double check and check again!

She never imagined herself to be the jealous type but Ava brought out the worst in her. She'd seen herself in one light—a good daughter, friend, dedicated employee, when she was employed, but now she felt like a green-eyed harpy.

And a sex maniac.

She couldn't wait for Gisele to wake up and distract her.

CHAPTER 31

A cold shower wouldn't be enough. Perhaps jumping naked off an Arctic polar cap would be better. But he'd burn up by the time he got there.

Max picked up the head of his fork and gripped it, feeling the tines bite into his palm. Why had she told him that dream—no, she'd called it a nightmare.

Why had he listened? Why had he...he'd lost his mind. Truly. When it came to her, he was never himself. He either came on too strong or too weak. She made him do ridiculous things like share his own fantasies. Except, unlike hers, it wasn't nightmarish at all.

He never imagined her in a towel or wrapped in sheets. When he allowed his thoughts to wander she was always...always wrapped around him. Completely. Legs, arms, clinging close to him and it felt good. She felt good. She smelled good too. And she didn't whisper his name. She said it in a low soft purr. Like a satisfied cat. She was soft and warm and she wanted him. She was always hungry for him. Her eyes would meet his and he'd sigh, pretending to be exhausted, but he wasn't and she'd pout and she'd kiss his cheek and then he'd kiss much more

Max closed his eyes, desperate to shift his thoughts. Yes, he was on a polar cap and he was cold. So cold and he felt human again. Except...except the polar cap was melting and it wasn't due to atmospheric interference. It was her.

Desiree.

She was there in a hot red towel (he really shouldn't have asked for that detail) and she was coming towards him and the closer she got the more the cap melted until suddenly he was surrounded by water and then it was covering his head. He was drowning and he didn't care.

He didn't care at all.

"Yes, Mom she's fine. You'll see her soon. No, I haven't told her anything yet," she lied.

Desiree was happy to be back at her apartment away from both the Fortunes and the Duchamps. She'd return to the Fortune house Monday to help Rudy with his last week of classes and then her job was finished. For now she needed space. She could feel like a human again, back in her own apartment. But then she'd called her mother to check in on her and her mother's questions seemed never ending. She'd asked about Ava non-stop for nearly an hour.

"And she looks happy?"

"She's fine," Desiree said putting her dirty clothes in a hamper. "She's well-fed. Great clothes. Lots of money."

"Did she say anything about Walter?"

"Who?"

"My ex."

"He seems to be out of the picture. Mom, it's going to be fine. She's lived a good life. She didn't suffer. She somehow found out about her father's lie and was looking for you. She'll be happy when she discovers the truth. She lived most of her life in Canada. She likes comic books."

"Which one?"

Desiree closed the hamper then frowned. "I don't know."

"You have to find out for me."

Desiree left her bedroom and sat on the couch. "You'll soon find out for yourself."

"But I could make a present of it. Wouldn't that be a wonderful surprise? Please, dear."

She sighed. "Fine."

"Thank you. You don't know how much this means."

"Right." She hung up. Ava was soon to gain a doting mother while she'd lost a friend.

She'd avoided Rachelle, ignoring her texts and calls until Rachelle surprised her by showing up on her doorstep with a pizza. She didn't have the heart to turn her away and knew that she couldn't share anything of what Max had told her.

To her annoyance she did have a good time with her, Rachelle was fun and easy to be with, but she also saw her in a new light. She noticed how causally she dropped hints about her tragic past and the cause, how easily she enjoyed insulting Max's character, career and family. This time Desiree didn't add fuel to the fire and Rachelle was openly disappointed.

"I guess you're getting on better with the Fortunes?"

Desiree set down her pizza slice and nodded. "And the Duchamps."

"Really?"

"Yes, while we were at Bethany Beach, I met Max's sister. I liked her." She decided not to share about knowing Gisele from before.

"She must have changed a lot then."

"I wouldn't know."

"Did you happen to see Max?"

"A little. I got a chance to know him a little better too."

"I see. I guess money can change ones impression of someone."

"And time. Time sometimes reveals a lot of things also."

Rachelle didn't know what to say to that and Desiree hadn't heard from her since. She hoped she'd taken the hint and wouldn't bother her anymore.

Now her mother wanted to give Ava, the woman who had everything, a present. A comic book.

At the beach house she'd briefly overheard Ava and Toyin discussing mangas (she'd at first thought they'd said mangos) and how one series was being turned into a live action feature. To her surprise Jackson had even joined them, talking about some series where the students were trying to assassinate the teacher. Personally Desiree thought it sounded ridiculous, but envied how easily Jackson and Toyin could talk to her.

If her mother wanted to give Ava a gift, she'd make

sure it was the best she could find. Fortunately, she knew that Toyin owned New Worlds a comic and pop culture store. Maybe she could give Desiree some suggestions and even get her a deal.

CHAPTER 33

Outside of a baseball field a woman carrying a wooden bat was rarely a good sign.

The day had started better than she'd hoped. When Desiree had gotten the idea to visit Toyin's store she'd half-expected to enter a dark place filled with nerdy men who had an obsession for fantasy women with big boobs and a passing acquaintance with personal hygiene.

But Toyin's store was warm and inviting.

Toyin greeted her with a big smile. She wore a silver wig and held a purple velvet witch costume with a deep V-neck front and flared sleeves. "Didn't know you were a fan," she said.

"I'm not really. I wanted to get something for Ava. That's quite an outfit."

Toyin frowned. "It's also something I can't sell. I'm displaying it on consignment for the local costume shop down the street. The woman's really nice but her business is struggling. However, this piece is taking up space. It's yours if you want it."

"How much does it cost?"

"I'll cover it. Don't worry."

Desiree looked over the outfit with interest; with some alteration she could make use of it. "Really?"

"Sure. Pop it in your trunk then come back and I'll get one of my clerks to help you with what you're looking for."

As promised, even though Desiree didn't know a lot about the comic industry, the clerk didn't make her feel like an imbecile and patiently answered her questions. In the background she overheard two people discussing why Batman wore a mask and Superman did not (something to do with the fact that one was an ordinary man and the other a good looking alien she stopped listening when they got into a heated argument about the kryptonic significance of Clark Kent's glasses). She'd learned the type of dedicated manga reader Ava was (Desiree didn't even know there were different categories and genres) and was directed to that section.

She was still there when she looked up and saw the woman.

Desiree stood facing the window in front of the parking lot and saw a tall woman get out of a car and head towards the shop entrance. She wore a mask of rage.

Desiree had a sinking feeling this wasn't someone playing a character from one of the comics. She turned to Toyin who was talking to a customer. "Um...this doesn't look good. I think we need to call the police."

But before anyone could move the woman barged into the store like the leader of a SWAT team and said, "Who's the owner here?"

Toyin stepped forward. "I am. If you'd like to step over here—"

"Are you proud of yourself? Proud of the lies and filth you distribute to our children?"

"I don't—"

The woman swung the bat and toppled a display. "This garbage!" She swung and knocked over a book shelf. "My son died because of you." Another stack of books and DVDs fell. She then dropped the bat and lunged at Toyin. "This is all your fault!"

They fell to the ground and the tall woman attacked Toyin like a wild animal.

Desiree grabbed pepper spray out of her handbag and sprayed the woman. The woman reeled back and covered her eyes. Desiree hoped to restrain her, but the woman broke free. She jumped up and stumbled out the front door.

Desiree fell on her knees beside Toyin. "Are you okay?" she asked, which was a silly question because she didn't look okay. She looked bloodied and scared.

"I will be in a minute." Toyin touched her bruised cheek and winced.

Desiree pulled out her cell phone.

Toyin stopped her. "We don't need the police. I'm not going to press charges. The woman seemed genuinely upset."

"She's crazy," Desiree said. "You can't let someone like that get away with what she just did."

"Let's clean up this mess. Briefly close. Make sure everyone's safe." She slowly stood and looked at the remainder of the people who hadn't run out of the store. "Everyone go home, I'll deal with this." She turned to Desiree. "Could you call Ava for me? She'll know what to do."

"Are you sure the police—"

"We have private security. They'll be on it."

"But she's already gone."

"They can look at the CCTV footage and take it from there. Thanks to Jackson I have a new state of the art security system installed. Trust me. Ava is my best option right now."

Desiree didn't want to call Ava, but was in no position to argue. She dialed and tensed when Ava picked up.

"Ava Hughes Fortune..."

Desiree cleared her throat. "I'm sorry to bother you, but..."

"What's wrong? Your voice sounds funny."

"It's Toyin. She asked me to call you. She got attacked

by—"

"Is she at the hospital?"

"No, she's still at the store." Desiree lowered her voice. "But she looks bad."

"Let me speak to someone on the security team."

Desiree looked around confused. What security team? "No one has arrived yet."

She heard Ava swear before she said, "I'll be right there."

~

When Ava arrived about ten minutes later she looked furious. "They're still not here?"

Desiree frowned. She'd left Toyin to rest in her office at the back of the store, but no one else was there. "Who?"

Before Ava could reply, a black Mazda drove up and an official looking man jumped out. The man couldn't even take a step before Ava pounced on him. Desiree couldn't hear what Ava was saying but she saw the man wither under her words. She pointed to the store and then to her watch. The man hung his head. Ava said a few more words before she returned to Desiree. "Tell Toyin I'm here and bring her to the car."

"Should I help her close up?"

Ava gestured to the two men entering the store. "No, these idiots will do the rest."

Minutes later Desiree sat beside Toyin in the back-seat while Ava drove. She'd come back for her car later, but she didn't want to leave Toyin alone. Toyin couldn't stop shaking.

Ava glanced back at her with concern. "I should probably take you—"

"I'm fine really," Toyin said. "Just shocked."

"I can't believe she came at you with a bat!"

"But she didn't hit me with it, thank goodness. Most of the damage was done to the store. It was her fists I couldn't escape. I feel like such a wimp. I couldn't get her to stop. If Desiree hadn't scared her off it would have been worse. Maybe I need to take some boxing lessons from Edgar."

Desiree knew it was Toyin's attempt at humor but Ava didn't smile. She patted Toyin's arm. "I think you got some choice blows in as well. Don't be so hard on yourself."

Toyin sighed. "Thanks."

"I still think we should have called the police."

When both women remained silent she realized she'd touched a delicate topic. One she didn't understand. What was so important about their special security anyway? "Or maybe not," she muttered.

"Where's James?" Toyin asked.

"Still at the office," Ava said.

"You didn't tell him—"

"No, I didn't see him. I came right after Desiree called me." She briefly glanced at Toyin in the rearview mirror then softly swore. "Jackson is going to flip out."

"Does he have to know?"

"You're joking, right?" When Toyin didn't respond, she sighed. "I don't think—"

"If we get to your house before James gets home, you could help me with some makeup. We could stop by a store and get the right shade."

"Half of your face is swollen."

"I only need a couple hours to get the swelling down. I'll rest in one of the rooms. No one needs to know that I'm there. Please Ava." She nudged Desiree. "Help me convince her."

Desiree thought she'd have a better chance of convincing a fish to breathe air, but Toyin seemed desperate. "She really needs a place to rest and I did work at a hospital and I can help look after her. I don't think she needs anymore stress right now."

"Fine," Ava said. "We'll do it your way for now. But you'll have to tell him eventually."

"Maybe he won't find out."

"That will be impossible."

CHAPTER 34

Max prided himself on not losing his temper. But as he stood in one of the shambled aisles in New Worlds, battered cardboard and scattered books beneath his feet, he could feel his control unraveling. He shouldn't be here. He shouldn't have to see this. Things shouldn't have happened the way they had.

He left the aisle and went to look at the security footage.

He looked over the CCTV camera three times unable to believe what he'd seen the first two. His heart was in his throat when he saw Desiree spring into action. She could have gotten hurt, but she didn't seem to care. That was the kind of woman she was. He wished he'd been there. He wished he could have taken that woman's bat and smashed her windscreen.

He took a deep breath then turned away from the

screens and faced his head manager of operations—Topper Carson.

A man he'd once thought of promoting, and now wanted to make cry like a toddler wearing a soggy diaper.

Max had always wondered why he'd hesitated with giving him a higher position. Finally he knew the reason. Topper wasn't loyal.

Top clients liked him. That had been a plus. He had a sharp, imposing presence that made people nervous. In security that was helpful. People in their industry didn't care about being liked; they wanted people to know that when things went south they had someone to depend on. MD Defense was supposed to be that kind of company.

Today Topper had proven them wrong.

"A woman with a can of pepper spray," Max said. "A woman with a can of pepper spray did a better job than the security team hired to guard this place."

"We did everything—"

He stopped when Max held up his hand. "Lying to me will only make it worse."

"If I'd known Jackson Fortune was the client, I—"

Max counted to ten. Topper was making it worse. Yes, this was the reason he couldn't take him higher in the ranks. He knew that the little shop seemed unprepossessing compared to some of the bigger clients they had. He'd kept the true owner private, because it shouldn't matter. It had been a test for Topper. But in the end it was MD Defense that had failed.

After liars. He hated failure.

Max took Topper's silk blue tie and smoothed it. "You shouldn't have had to know who the true client was." He brushed imaginary lint from his shoulder, Max could feel him trembling. "Do you know why?"

Topper shook his head.

"Because when I tell you to do something, I expect you to do it to your utmost ability. I don't care if I ask you to outfit a trailer or someone's cat carrier. If I say do it, you do it. You do not question my choices; you do not shame my name by doing a half-assed job."

"I'm sorry. I'll fix it."

"How?"

"I already have someone looking into identifying the woman. We'll—"

"No, I mean how will you regain my trust?"

Topper faltered.

Max nodded. "You know where the exit is. Good-bye." He turned to Holland. "You know what to do with him." Dismissals of this sort had to be done with the utmost care and caution.

"Should I call Jackson?"

"No," Max said in a grim tone. "I have a feeling, he'll be calling me."

CHAPTER 35

"*W*here is she!"

Ava inwardly groaned as the peaceful atmosphere she'd been enjoying in the great room was shattered by the sound of Jackson's voice in the foyer. She calmly set her manga aside and stood. Jackson could venture on the theatrics, but by his bellowing voice she knew two things. One: somehow he'd found out what had happened to Toyin faster than she'd thought he would and two: he was livid.

She walked into the hallway. "Do you need to shout?"

"Where is she?"

"Jackson calm down. What's going on?"

He narrowed his eyes. "Don't pretend you don't know. Where is Toyin?"

"She's resting. Although I'm not sure she is anymore. Desiree is looking after her." She turned.

Jackson grabbed her arm and spun her back to face him. "When were you going to tell me?"

Ava yanked her arm away. "Later."

He rested his hands on his hips. "I know we don't always see eye to eye but this is beneath you." He held out his cell phone. "Do you want to know why I'm here? Because I got a frantic call from a clerk at Toyin's shop. I didn't understand why she sounded so upset until she tells me she's worried because Toyin wasn't answering her phone and she's been trying to reach her for almost *two hours*! She wanted to know if Toyin got home safe. Do you know why she asked me that?"

"Jackson—"

"Because a crazy woman with a baseball bat attacked her."

"Thankfully," Ava said in a calm, steady voice, "she didn't hit her with it. Most of the damage happened to the displays."

"What about security?"

She turned away to head back to her book. "Give her time to rest."

"Ava."

She paused. She didn't want to talk about it, but he deserved to know the truth. She slowly turned back to him. "I gave him a piece of my mind. They arrived the same time I did. I'm sorry. I did what I could. She didn't want to tell you until—"

Jackson's tone hardened. "I won't ask you a fourth time."

Ava sighed. She would let Jackson have his way. She'd

seen him angry before but nothing like this. As she led him to the room where Toyin was resting, she wanted to dart ahead and cover her up, but Jackson marched ahead. He opened the door and Ava saw Toyin sitting up in bed sketching while Desiree made a funny pose for her. Both women turned to the door surprised, but Ava knew Jackson only saw one face.

Toyin's face.

And it didn't look good.

For a second he looked like he was about to cry. He stared at his wife with the same dejected horror of a little boy who'd just seen his beloved teddy bear get its head ripped off. Then the lost boy expression was quickly replaced by that of a man. A man filled with rage. "She will be destroyed," he said. And his words were a promise. He turned to the door.

"Jackson don't," Toyin called after him.

"I will annihilate her."

Toyin rushed over to him and grabbed his arm. "Jackson, come back here."

He paused then slowly turned. He lifted a trembling hand to her face then let it fall before he touched her. "I will destroy her."

"No, you don't have to do that. She's disturbed. Let the—"

"I will find her and make her hurt so bad she'll want to die. Don't worry, I won't lay a finger on her. I promise you that, my darling."

"Jackson, she's a woman in grief—"

He gently led her back to the bed. "Rest and don't worry about anything."

"Jackson, please don't—"

He kissed her hand before he drew away from her. "I'll see you later." He turned to Ava. "Send me the pictures," he said before he left.

Toyin looked at Ava frantic. "You have to stop him."

"I don't think I can." Jackson was sharp enough to know that Ava would have taken pictures of Toyin's bruises for documentation.

She pulled out her cell phone and called her husband. "James, I need you to call your brother right now and stop him from doing something he might regret."

James laughed amused. "Have I ever managed to do that?"

"This is serious."

His good humor died. "What's going on?"

"I can't explain it all now, but please call him this instant. At least let him talk to you." She disconnected and looked at Toyin then Desiree. "You know this is now bigger than all of us right?"

"What about Edgar?" Toyin asked. "If Jackson's upset, Edgar might be worse. You know how he feels about family."

"Maybe I should go home," Toyin said.

"I think you should rest a little longer. Which is what you were supposed to be doing," she said sending Desiree a look of displeasure. "Why were you sketching?"

"I had to do something. Every time I closed my eyes I saw that woman's face and it kept me up. I thought of some moves, I thought of myself as cooler than I am. I'm embarrassed. I couldn't have fought her and if Desiree hadn't come—"

"But she did. And you did the right thing keeping your employees and patrons safe."

"I'll go in tomorrow to see the true damage."

"No, you won't."

"People get punched all the time. I'm not the first. I have to stand tall. People depend on me."

"One or two days won't make a difference," Desiree said. "Rest the remainder of the week. James will talk to both Jackson and Edgar, the culprit will be caught and dealt with and everything will be okay."

Ava shook her head. "If you truly think that then you're naïve."

"What do you think will happen?"

Ava folded her arms. "That's the problem, I have no idea."

CHAPTER 36

James stared at his cell phone not understanding his wife's cryptic message. But her voice sounded urgent. Getting his brother out of trouble had become a second job, stopping him from causing it would be a first. He rang his brother a little surprised when Jackson quickly picked up.

"I need you to help me," Jackson said.

"Help you do what?"

He gave James a briefing of what had happened at Toyin's store. James softly swore.

"I need to find her," Jackson said. "I need to know how to make her hurt when I do find her and I need it to be swift and painful. But first I need you to contact Max."

"I'm sure—"

"I'm not sure of anything. Ava said the security detail arrived when she did. How is that possible?"

James didn't know but none of this sounded good. "Let's think this through."

"That's why I am talking to you and not—" He stopped and started again. "You're the thinker. Tell me what to do otherwise I have a plan of my own. You deal with Max and I'll deal with this bitch."

"Jackson, listen—"

"Before you say anything else I want you to look at something." Jackson sent the pictures Ava had taken of Toyin's bruises.

James looked at the images on his screen, rubbed his forehead and swore again.

"Don't tell me to do nothing."

"I won't."

He could feel his brother's anger and it mingled with his own. Someone hadn't just attacked his brother's wife. They'd attacked James's family. He felt the violation, the rage. Someone had hurt one of their own. They couldn't let that pass lightly. "Okay, I'll talk to Max, but for now I want you to do exactly as I say..."

To Ava's surprise Edgar didn't say anything at dinner. He didn't ask why Jackson and Toyin had decided to join them. He barely blinked an eye when Rudy said, "What happened to your face?" and Toyin told him that something happened at work.

Edgar took a sip of his drink, asked some pointed questions about work before he finished his meal and left the table. Ava didn't dare catch anyone's eye knowing they were all thinking the same thing—they could keep what had happened between them. Edgar didn't want to get involved. She was about to release a sigh of relief when James then Jackson both excused themselves at the same time. That was a bad sign. The men were up to something and they didn't want them knowing about it.

Once they were gone, Toyin glanced at the door and said, "Go and listen."

Ava frowned. "Absolutely not."

Toyin turned to Desiree. "How about you?"

When Desiree started to stand, Ava said, "Sit down. None of us are going to eavesdrop on their conversation."

Desiree sat back in her chair.

"But they're up to something," Toyin said.

"Of course they are. But don't worry I plan to find out what it is."

Desiree stood up again. "And I want to do one last review with Rudy before I have some errands I need to run." She hesitated feeling like a kid asking permission to go outside and play. "If that's okay."

"That's fine," Ava said with a curt nod. "As long as you understand—"

"Don't worry, I won't breathe a word about what happened to anyone."

"Thank you."

Toyin smiled at her. "Yes, thanks for everything."

Once they were alone, Toyin said, "You can trust her, you know."

"Who?"

"Desiree. She really was great at the store and when I

was moping she was the one who suggested I sketch so that I could feel better. I know you wanted me to rest, but that helped me even more. I don't know why you dislike her."

Ava looked at her surprised. "I never said that."

"You don't have to. You're very...distant with her."

Ava bristled at the thought. She may not have been chummy with Desiree but she didn't think she'd given any indication that she disliked her. Desiree could be a little too friendly, and she'd regretted being curt with her when Desiree had talked about James. But since then she'd felt she'd been perfectly cordial. "It's nothing personal. I just have a lot on my mind."

And right now all she could think about was what Edgar, James and Jackson were scheming. That night as she sat in bed and watched James change for bed she asked him, "What are you thinking of doing? You know you have to tell me."

"It's better that I don't."

"We agreed not to keep secrets from each other."

James slid into bed beside her. "Said the woman who didn't tell me that she left the office to pick up our sister-in-law who'd been attacked."

"I didn't have time to tell you. I wasn't hiding anything."

"We're going to find this woman and then...let her know the error of her ways."

"Toyin won't like that."

"She doesn't have a choice."

"I think you shouldn't do anything. With Jackson comes trouble."

"Someone attacked his wife. I don't want to stop him. I'm as angry as he is."

"So am I but you might make matters worse by going down the road of revenge."

He sent her a significant look. "Are you speaking from experience?"

She narrowed her eyes. "No."

He shrugged. "It's not about revenge. However, that's why I'm staying involved. I'll make sure Jackson doesn't take it too far."

"What did Edgar say?"

James hesitated. "*That* I can't tell you."

"Why not?"

"I don't think I've heard so many curse words strung together in my life."

Ava saw the shock on James's face and couldn't stop a giggle. "He was that mad?"

"Mad isn't the right word."

"Did you talk to Max?"

James nodded. "I did."

"What did he say after he apologized?"

"How do you know he apologized?"

"His security was a complete cock-up. I'd expect him to."

"He did and let's just say he has his way of doing things and we have ours. It will be perfectly legal."

"Then why does the thought of you finding this woman make me nervous?"

A cold dark look entered his eyes. "Because it should. We will make sure she knows that messing with the Fortunes comes with consequences."

"Promise me—"

"No."

Toyin sat back in defeat as she sat in the passenger's seat of Jackson's red Porsche. They'd spent most of the drive in silence, Jackson refusing to tell her what he'd talked about with his stepfather and brother. Even though it was nearly eight o'clock in the evening, the summer sun still shone bright in a cloudless blue sky overhead.

However, the tension she sensed within Jackson made her think of a coming rainstorm. She'd never seen him this tense. Fortunately, the event had happened so fast that only two shaky recordings of the event had popped up online and hadn't been interesting or brutal enough to gain traction.

"I'm a grown woman and you're treating me like a child. Let me—"

"No."

"I recently read a story about a kid who killed himself when a beloved character in his favorite anime died. I think this woman must have been his mother and wanted someone to blame, but I don't think she'll come back."

"I will make sure of it."

"You can't hurt her."

He shot her a look. "I don't hit women. Unless they strike first." He gripped the steering wheel. "I hope she gives me a reason."

"You don't need—"

"Stop."

"What?"

"Stop trying to convince me to do nothing. Stop trying to make this all okay. It's not. It's not okay that someone attacked your store and you and then fled the scene. I don't care what their reasons are. I don't care if they lost their family in a massacre. She will know that it's not okay to mess with the Fortunes. And it's certainly not okay that the security I paid for failed you."

"I CAN'T REACH HIM."

Desiree glanced at the screen on her cell phone to make sure she'd seen the right phone number and name. She'd just left Rudy's room and was heading down the stairs to pick up something at the store when her cell phone rang. It said 'Gisele' on the screen but the slurred voice on the other end didn't sound like her. She heard a crowd in the background. It sounded like a party. "I think you have the wrong number."

"Max. I can't reach Max."

Desiree stopped before she disconnected. "Gisele, have you been drinking?"

"Not much. Just a little," she said except her words sounded like 'mush' and 'lickle.'

She walked past the closed library door, briefly curious what was going on there, before she walked outside. "Sounds like more than a little."

"He promised we'd go out and then he changed his mind. I called Holland."

"Holland?"

"You know, his assistant."

She knew he had an assistant, but never got his name. She headed over to her car. "Right."

"Yea, I called him to find out what was going on and he said my brother is fuming! That if Max could lift a house and throw it he would. He told me to keep my distance for now and stay out of his way."

She unlocked her car and sat inside. "That might be a good idea."

"But I'm worried about him. I really am. I saw a bruise on his palm and he told he didn't know how he got it. That's not like him. He hasn't been the same since the beach house."

Desiree felt guilty that she couldn't tell her friend why. "I'm sure he's fine."

"No, that's where you're wrong. Everybody's always wrong about him." She sounded like she wanted to cry.

"Gisele," Desiree said suddenly alarmed. She remembered how depressed Gisele had been in the hospital all those years ago. And Max had mentioned how she still struggled with anxiety. "Is there anyone with you? I mean someone special," she clarified because from the noise in the background she knew she wasn't by herself.

"No, I came here to think."

"Okay, but I think you've done enough thinking. Promise me you won't drive. Call a...never mind tell me where you are and I'll come get you."

But getting inside the exclusive club was easier said than done. When the bouncer saw her, giving her worn jeans and T-shirt a disparaging look, he told her the club had a dress code. She tried to tell him she didn't plan to stay but had a friend inside. "I'm a friend of Gisele Duchamp."

"Right," the guard sneered. "And I'm with the Secret Service."

"It's true. I—"

"Do you have her number?"

"Yes."

"Then you can call her to come and meet you out here," he said.

Which she tried to do, but Gisele wouldn't pick up her phone. Desiree looked around and noticed a truck pulled up to the back loading dock and saw people carrying boxes inside and came up with an idea.

She went back to her car, changed into the dress she'd gotten at Toyin's shop, it fit a little tighter than she would have liked but at least it fit, then raced back to the loading area since she didn't think the bouncer in the front would approve of her new outfit either.

She quickly grabbed one of the boxes, taking one large enough to cover most of her, and snuck inside.

She then left the box in the hallway and made her way to the first level lured by the sound of loud music. When she opened the door, flashing lights pounded on the dance floor and the crush of people. She made her way to the second level where private tables circled around the room. Then she saw the executive level and had a sneaking suspicions she'd find Gisele there.

But when a security person saw her, she blocked her path. "I'm the entertainment," Desiree said as she gestured to her costume. "Gisele Duchamp is expecting me."

The woman looked Desiree up and down, took a quick picture of her before she said, "Wait here," and disappeared behind the door. Moments later she returned and said, "Go on. She's in the third room."

Desiree walked through the door and felt like she was entering a new world. The music behind her became muted, the lights faded into a grey wall and marble floor. She stopped in front of the third room, opened the door and saw an elegant suite with a private bar, large table where crystals appeared to rain down from a waterfall chandelier stationed above the U-shaped array of gray cushioned chairs.

She found Gisele fast asleep on one of them.

Desiree nudged her awake.

Gisele looked up at her with a sleepy smile, but Desiree didn't smell a lot of liquor on her. "You made it." Her gaze fell to Desiree's dress. She squinted. "Why are you all dressed up?"

Because I had to sneak inside here. She also noticed Gisele's words weren't as slurred as they'd seemed over the phone. "I'll tell you later and now it's time to go home."

Fortunately, getting Gisele back to the second level wasn't difficult until she got distracted by the light and raced to the railing to see the people dancing below.

"Wanna dance?"

"No."

"Don't you like to dance?"

"We're going home," Desiree started to say before she saw a familiar face sitting in one of the private booths. Rachelle. Looking radiant in a black dress, a man, no doubt wealthy enough to afford the table, pushed her hair away from her face. She grabbed Gisele's arm hoping she wouldn't see her, but she was too late.

She gasped. "What's she doing here?"

"Come on, let's go."

"She's not supposed to be..." Gisele started to shake, her face a mask of horror as if she were recalling that doomed trip to Mexico with Rachelle and all the surgeries she'd had to suffer afterwards. "Oh God now I know why Max has been so upset," she said surprising Desiree with her theory. "She's hurting him again. I have to tell Max. Or maybe he doesn't know yet. I have to warn him." She grabbed Desiree's arm and headed for the elevator. "We have to go."

"Where?"

"To see Max."

CHAPTER 38

"Well?" Toyin asked when she called Ava later that evening. She sat alone in her art studio, a black and white line drawing for her web cartoon on her computer monitor. She lifted the stylus of her digital sketchpad to select a color and fill in the background. Since she hadn't been able to get anything from Jackson she'd hoped Ava had had better luck with James.

Ava sighed. "James said that they would find the woman and put a little fear in her and that would be it."

"Do you believe him?"

"I don't think he'd lie to me about that."

"I've never seen Jackson so upset."

"Can you blame him?"

"No, but I feel as if I should have handled it better." She set her stylus down and sat back in her chair. "I should have calmed her down."

"You did nothing wrong and don't let him hear you say that, it will make him even angrier."

"I know. Thanks for coming to get me. I didn't know who else to call."

"We're family. It's what we do."

Toyin hesitated. "Are you ready to meet her?"

"Who?"

"Your mother."

Ava paused. "Sort of."

"I'm sure it will be great."

"Right."

"And Desiree seems nice."

Ava laughed. "You already said that before. You don't have to sell her to me you know."

"I know, but you're still worried about something."

"No, I still don't know how to feel."

"Well, if you need to talk. I'm here."

"I could have strangled you today."

"Why?"

"I'd hoped you'd be in the bed covered up and then I could had lied to Jackson and said you needed more rest instead I see you sitting up with a swollen face sketching like nothing had happened."

"I told you, Desiree—"

"It's okay, I've gotten used to things not turning out the way I'd planned."

Toyin fell silent for a moment before she said, "Do you ever feel like they regret it?"

"Regret what?"

"Getting married? I know that James loves you and Jackson—"

"Jackson wouldn't have married you if he didn't want

to. He is only trying to remind you that you can't act like you have in the past."

"But I need him to know he can trust me. That I'm not a burden."

"I know he doesn't see you that way."

"It feels that way all the same."

Ava sighed. "Stop worrying and get some rest."

"Okay."

Ava disconnected the phone then was alerted to another message. A message she'd both hoped for and dreaded.

CHAPTER 39

He wished he hadn't opened the door.

Max took one look at the sight of his tipsy sister on Desiree's arm outside his apartment and realized that one of the worse days of his life was about to get even worse.

"I'm sorry about this, but she insisted on seeing you," Desiree said at the same time Gisele lunged at her brother, grabbed his collar and said, "I saw her. She's here."

Max looked at Desiree in question.

"She saw Rachelle in the club."

Max ushered them both inside and closed the door. "I see."

"She's here," Gisele said again with more urgency. "You have to protect yourself. She's dangerous."

"I know."

Her eyes widened. "Did you see her too? Did you talk to her? Is that why you're unhappy?" She started to shake. "She's going to hurt us. She'll take you away from me. She's out to destroy—"

He cupped his sister's face in his hands. "No," he said in a firm voice. "I would never let that happen."

Her shaking increased and she started to cry. "But she can-"

"You're safe. I'll—"

"How can I protect you?" She fell to the ground and buried her face in her hands. "She'll—"

"It will be okay," Max said in a gentle voice before he lifted his sister in his arms. He looked at Desiree. "Don't go anywhere." He left and disappeared down the hall.

Desiree didn't move. Too afraid to. She was in Max's apartment. His lair. And it wasn't what she'd expected. She wasn't exactly sure what she'd expected (black furniture, steel numb chucks and machetes on the wall perhaps) but instead the place looked so normal. Worse, it made him human.

The letter he'd given her made him seem flawed.

The dream she'd had of him made him seem sexy.

But she hadn't seen him as human before.

A human who lived in a gorgeous penthouse suite in a building he owned, but a human nonetheless. He looked so ordinary dressed in jeans and a dark red, fully zipped hoodie with the words *MD Defense* blazoned across it.

He came out of the other room.

"Thanks for..." He rested his hands on his hips and sighed. "She still has panic attacks. I'm sorry about this."

"It's okay. It's the perfect end to an equally awful day."

He nodded.

She looked at him surprised. "You too?"

He nodded again.

"Want to compare notes?"

He shook his head.

"Okay. I should go."

"No, don't do that. Not yet at least. She might want to see you. Give her a few minutes."

"Okay." Desiree looked around again, her eyes falling on the distinct wall art, warm grey-green walls, and furnishing that appeared more cultivated than bought to impress before she turned to him surprised to see him studying her.

She could sense him waiting, which also surprised her. Did he really care what she thought about his place? He didn't seem the type. She folded her arms. "May I sit down?"

He gestured to the couch. "Of course."

She did and looked around again. "This place is...great."

He still didn't move, he watched her, wary.

"Are you going to stand there?"

He folded his arms. "For now. Want anything to eat? Drink?"

"No."

"I'm going to check on..." He gestured to the hall as if he'd forgotten his sister's name. "I'll be right back."

"Okay." Desiree watched him leave, confused. If she didn't know him better she would have thought he seemed a little flustered. But he must be very concerned about his sister.

She picked up a magazine about security from off his coffee table accidentally knocking a pen to the ground that rolled under the couch. She bent down to pick it up and saw two eyes staring back at her.

She gasped and jumped up. What the heck was that? Did she imagine it? She cautiously bent down to check again, the eyes blinked and she heard the sound of claws scurrying backwards. Of course! He had a pet. She'd nearly forgotten about that.

"It's okay. I'm not going to hurt you. Do you have treats?" she wondered. The dog didn't move.

She heard Max's footsteps returning. She sat on the couch pretending nothing had happened. He stood behind her. "Are you sure you're not thirsty?"

"I'm fine." He still looked tense, but now she knew why. He wasn't worried about how she was responding to his place; he was worried about his dog. She'd take him out of his misery.

"What's its name?" she asked, pretending she didn't know.

"Hmm?"

"You either have an animal under this couch or the biggest dust bunny I've ever seen."

Max came from behind the couch. "That's where he is? I was looking everywhere. I forgot about here."

Desiree bent in front of the couch. "He's here."

Max joined her. "What are you doing?"

"Trying to get him to come out. What is he exactly?" she asked curious to see what Max would tell her.

Max looked at her then quickly looked away, embarrassed. "A cowardly dog."

"Just a little scared."

Max kept his gaze forward as if trying to avoid looking at her. "The most cowardly dog I've ever met."

She found his discomfort amusing. "How do you get him to come out of hiding?"

"I usually just lift up the couch and he scrambles out."

"Have you tried coaxing him with treats?"

"No. I..." His voice faded and he turned away.

"What?"

"It's stupid."

"Whatever works."

Max sent her a long look. "You cannot tell anyone about this."

"Who would I tell?"

"James, Jackson, Ava, Edgar—"

Desiree waved her hand. "Okay, okay, fine. I won't say anything."

"Promise."

"I promise."

Max unzipped his hoodie halfway then tapped his chest. "Come on. It's safe." In seconds the little dog–it turned out to be a Jack Russell Terrier mutt—scrambled out from under the couch and jumped on his chest then curled itself up.

"Aw," Desiree said, "he's like a baby kangaroo going into its mother's pouch."

"He's an embarrassment."

"How did you get him to do that?"

"I...uh...don't know where he got it from, but my former housekeeper used to own him and when she passed I inherited him. I guess he learned it from her."

"That's sweet." She scratched the top of the dog's head. "Look, he's smiling."

"No, that's his typical stupid expression."

"I can't believe you have a pet like this. I thought you'd have an expensive breed. No I didn't think you'd own one at all." She bent close and let the dog lick her nose.

Max stiffened and abruptly took the dog out from under his hoodie and set him on the couch.

"Won't he hide again?"

"No, he's fine now." He stood, shoving in hands in his pockets. "Usually he's shaking, but he's calm. He likes you."

"You don't sound pleased."

He hesitated. "I...don't trust my judgment anymore. I trusted someone I shouldn't have and mistrusted someone I should have trusted."

Desiree sat beside the dog and stroked it. "Is that why you lied?"

"Lied?"

"I know this dog's name is AP for Abandoned Puppy because you found him on the side of the road and adopted him. Your sister told me the entire story." She looked up at him with a sly grin. "My question is, why didn't you?"

Max rubbed the back of his neck. "She talks too much."

"I like her story better. Why did you lie?"

"I lied because..." He let his hands fall to his side,

shook his head, glanced at the clock, then the hallway, before looking at her again. "You sure you don't want something to eat?"

"I'm fine." She studied him. Was he really that worried about his sister? He wasn't acting like himself. She grabbed his hand. "Relax. Gisele just had too much to drink. She'll recover. Rachelle didn't see us."

He took a deep breath. "Thanks."

She released his hand surprised by how normal it had felt to hold. It felt warm, solid and oddly comforting. "You're welcome."

"You're always coming to her rescue. I'm sorry she ruined your party."

"Party?"

"Your dress."

Desiree glanced down and inwardly cringed. She'd forgotten about the costume she'd put on and the V-neck top was showing more cleavage than before. "I know I look ridiculous."

"No, actually—"

"I wasn't at a party. I used this outfit to sneak inside the club to get Gisele because they wouldn't let me inside."

His gaze sharpened. "Which club?"

"I should remember the name, but I don't. All I know is she was in the VIP suite and getting to her took some cunning."

His expression changed. "Why didn't you tell the front that—"

"I tried that. Trust me. They didn't believe me and when I called her she wouldn't pick up so I changed into this outfit and snuck through the back and pretended to be part of the entertainment. I didn't think the first bouncer would fall for my story if I went back to him so I had no choice."

Max swore. "You should have called me."

"I don't have your number."

"You could have gotten it from James."

"James already has a lot on him mind. But why would I call you, anyway?"

"Because it's one of our clubs. Gisele only goes there." He rubbed his forehead. "I don't believe this."

She shrugged. "It's okay."

His eyes clung to her and his voice deepened. "I really wish you'd called me."

The look in his eyes made her heart pick up pace. Was he angry at her for sneaking inside his club? "I didn't mean—"

"Better yet, I wish you'd come to me dressed like that and...Never mind. I wouldn't want to give you night-mares again."

"Nightmares?"

"About me."

She frowned. Why was he bringing that up now? "I don't understand."

He nodded and sighed. "I know."

"Then tell me. What did I do wrong now?"

"Nothing." He hung his head. "I lied about AP because I wanted to impress you."

"I like the original story."

"Makes me sound soft."

She shook her head. "No, it doesn't."

His eyes darkened with emotion. "Really?"

She shivered, strangely flattered that he cared. His intense gaze gave her goose bumps.

He frowned. "Are you cold?" He took off his hoodie and wrapped it around her shoulders.

It felt warm and smelled like citrus. She stared at him amazed as she put it on. "I didn't think guys really did this in real life."

He grinned. "Well, I don't need it and it's great for brand marketing."

She looked down and remembered that *MD Defense* was splashed across it. "You were supposed to leave the last part out."

His grin widened.

Desiree gasped and mimed holding up a microphone before she said in the voice of a British announcer from a nature documentary, "This is a rare and extraordinary sight indeed. The illusive creature maximillius duchampanus has actually smiled. That we were here to witness such an amazing event is truly incredible."

He folded his arms. "Very funny." He hesitated. "I know what you think of me and most of it I deserve, but I'm not a monster."

"I know." She bit her lip before she said, "I lied too."

"About what?"

"About my dream."

"I wasn't in it?"

"No, I lied that I was afraid of you, but I wasn't afraid at all." She lowered her eyes. "The idea of being in your arms isn't a nightmare to me anymore."

His voice deepened to a husky whisper. "I don't believe you."

"I have no way to prove it."

"Yes, you do," he said then drew her to him and kissed her with tantalizing persuasion. She'd expected a man like him to be more demanding, aggressive, assertive, but his lips were teasing, almost playful daring her to pull away, daring her to breathe. But she didn't want to breathe. Until she'd kissed him she didn't realize she'd felt so cold, so alone. He not only made her hot and breathless, he made her hungry. Hungry for more. She deepened the kiss and let it quickly turn from playful exploration to a daring challenge called 'can you take the heat?'

She wasn't sure she could. His arms embraced her and his mouth became a master of manipulation toying with her senses, causing her to question everything she knew about herself and about him. She couldn't believe she was kissing him. Letting the sensation of his wet tongue enter her mouth and enjoying every wet second. She couldn't believe she was touching him, wrapping her arms around him and bringing her body close. Like a woman frozen coming close to a fire. So much heat. So much fire.

He drew away. "We should—"

"No." She kissed him again. She didn't want to think. She only wanted to feel. She wanted to feel this rush of sweet pleasure that coursed through her when their lips touched, when she felt the heat of his palm slid up her back and settle on her neck. She wanted to feel desired. She didn't care what he thought of her, she didn't care that this strange, wild moment at the end of an awful day wouldn't last. She needed it.

She needed it—him—so bad.

When she reached for the front of his T-shirt, Max covered her hands. "That's enough."

Desiree looked at him startled unable to read his face. Did he mean that he'd had enough of her? That it was all a game?

He lifted her hands and kissed them, a playful gleam in his eyes. "Somehow I knew you'd be dangerous."

"Me? Dangerous?"

He nodded. "Especially to me." He turned and headed for the front door. "Do you mind staying with Gisele for a couple more minutes? Thanks," he said not giving her a chance to reply before he left.

CHAPTER 40

*D*esiree stared at the closed door stunned. What had just happened? What was that? He kissed her and then just left?

"Did someone leave?" Gisele said, strolling into the room, rubbing her eyes. Her makeup was smudged and her hair all over the place, but at least she didn't look as miserable as she had been a few minutes ago.

"Max, he said he'd be back. How are you feeling?"

"Better."

Desiree studied her. Aside from her anxiety attack, she'd sobered up pretty quickly. "Why did you really call me?"

Gisele blinked, the face of innocence. "I told you. I was worried about Max."

Desiree suspected more but wouldn't press her. "Want me to make you something?"

She shrugged not giving her an answer one way or the other. "He's probably in his studio."

"Studio?"

"Yes," Gisele picked AP up and sat down in front of her. "He always goes there when he's upset about something. It's down the hall. You can't miss it."

"I see." But in fact she didn't and she really wanted to. She wanted to find out as much about him as she could. How could he find her dangerous when with one kiss he left her breathless? She couldn't get enough of him. Was he upset that he liked her?

She told herself it didn't matter. A kiss was just a kiss as the song said. She told Gisele she would be right back, then dashed to her car and changed back into her street clothes, remembering to slip back into the hoodie, before returning to the apartment.

She went into the kitchen. Gisele may not be hungry, but she needed something to do. Plus she was curious to see what a bachelor like Max kept in his kitchen.

It was well-stocked and organized. Likely due to his chef or housekeeper. She saw lots of fruits and vegetables as if he'd bought up half the produce section. Desiree quickly chopped up some carrots, celery and peppers, then she did the same to a mango, apple and kiwi, all the while thinking of why Max had disappeared to his studio. She kept reminding herself that it didn't matter. She made a dip from some spare ingredients then went back into the living room.

Gisele stared at the arrangement in shock. "What happened?"

It was when she asked that question that Desiree realized she'd gotten a little carried away. What she'd chopped up could have fed twenty people. Max wouldn't appreciate that she'd raided his fridge and chopped up half his produce. "I uh...wanted to make sure there would be enough for your brother."

A soft smile danced on Gisele's lips. "Then you'd better go tell him."

"No, you're looking better and I think I should—"

Gisele pointed to the door. "Go tell him. He hates food going to waste."

Desiree sighed then left the apartment and headed down the hall. She told herself that she was only searching him out to tell him about the food and because Gisele had insisted.

She knew it was a lie. She was lying to herself but she didn't care. She walked inside the studio, surprised by the size and space, the hardwood floor, bright lights and row of mirrors, she heard a sound but didn't see him at first. She ducked behind a sport machine, peeked out from behind it and saw him near the far wall.

And stared.

She was spying. She knew spying on him was wrong, underhanded, beneath her, but she couldn't help herself. She couldn't take her eyes off him. He was shirtless as he did intricate powerful moves in the center of the room. His body cut the air like a knife. He made her feel as if she could see sound, grasp air. She had no idea he was so strong. Did the bodies of all Brazilian jiu-jitsu experts look like this?

She envied his control. She could hardly stay still a second let alone thirty. She counted. How she wanted to hate him. How she wished she were a strong opponent. She briefly imagined going up against him. That would be fun. In her dreams she was a worthy opponent, taking him by surprise. Toppling him to the ground. Looking down on him in victory as he stared up at her in shock and awe. *No one has ever defeated me before,* he'd say. And she'd just smile and then he'd say...

"How long are you going to sit there staring at me with your mouth open?"

Desiree blinked, her thoughts bursting like a bubble. Her fantasy-Max wouldn't say that, but the real life version would. How did he know she was there? And she didn't have her mouth open? Did she? She bit her lip.

"Come on," he said with a note of amusement. "I won't pretend I don't see you."

If she stayed very still perhaps he'd question himself, perhaps he'd think her shadow was something else. Then she could dash out and return and act like a normal person.

"I can see you in the mirror."

Desiree briefly closed her eyes. The mirror! She'd forgotten about the stupid mirrors.

She sighed and came out of hiding. "I wasn't watching you. I wanted to tell you that I made some snacks and then I was looking around and I saw you and I didn't want to bother you so I—" She stopped talking, knowing she sounded ridiculous. She walked over to him. "I've always been impressed by the martial arts." As she got closer she felt relieved to see that he didn't look angry. He looked wary.

"So you hid and decided to watch me?" he said.

She nodded, trying not to look at his lips or his shoulders. Or his beautiful, muscular chest.

He folded his arms. "Want to try?"

She blinked. "Try?"

"You looked interested. You said you've always been impressed by the martial arts. I could show you a few moves."

"You're making fun of me."

"No, I'm not."

She looked down at herself in despair. He was built like a stone statue and she like a marshmallow. "I'm not exactly built—"

"You're built to move and that's what's important." He turned her to face the mirror before he stood behind her. "Your core is key." He rested his hands on her hips. "And many people underestimate the crucial capabilities of their hips."

He was hot and sweaty, she should be disgusted, but she wasn't. She was turned on.

"I'm going to show you a signature submission move or would you like me to show you one of the mount positions."

"Mount?"

"Yes, you lay flat with your legs wrapped around your opponent and a common mount defense would—"

She didn't care. She didn't know how she could continue to listen to him while he used words like 'submission' and 'mount' without thinking of him as everything except her opponent. Desiree spun away from him and waved her hands. "I can't do this."

He grinned. "Of course you can. I'll even let you subdue me."

How could he make that sound dirty? Why did she like it? "No."

"You're shy?"

"I'm scared."

He frowned. "I wouldn't hurt you."

"I know that." She rubbed her arms. "I'm sorry I bothered you. I only wanted you to know—"

His voice deepened. "I'm glad you came."

She poked his chest with her forefinger. "Then why did you run away?"

"I didn't run away."

"You left me."

He shook his head. "I gave you space. Before we go any further you need to be sure about me." He rested his hands on his hips and hung his head.

"I know you've been hurt. I've been hurt too."

He lifted his head, his eyes still unsure. "By me."

"Yes, but you weren't the only one." She held out her hand.

He hesitated. She could see the longing in his gaze but he didn't move. "I really messed up today. The security company that was supposed to guard Toyin's shop was mine."

"I know."

"And that doesn't bother you?"

"You'll fix it, right?"

"Of course but—"

"And you've made massive mistakes before like publicly humiliating a woman because she told a tiny lie."

He rubbed his chin and groaned. "Something I will never live down."

"Not anytime soon. But you can make it up to me." She wiggled her fingers. "Come on."

"I hate letting my friends down."

Before Desiree could respond her cell phone alerted her to a text. She looked down at the message and her throat tensed. It was time to stop pretending. She held the message up for him to see. It was the DNA result.

"This proves Ava and I are related. I've let my mother down all her life and now I've got a chance to make it right." She took his hand. "But even though I've gained a sister, I feel like I've also lost something."

He squeezed her hand. "I'm sure your mother loves you both equally."

That's what hurt the most, she couldn't tell him she knew that wasn't true.

CHAPTER 41

Tomorrow she'd meet her. It had been nearly a week since the DNA result that led to a flurry of phone calls and, as promised, James arranged everything.

Ava still wasn't ready, but there was no way to stop what was about to happen. She fell on her knees and searched between the mattress and bed frame. She couldn't find the knife. Had she dropped it somewhere? Left it somewhere? She looked under the bed, inside the bathroom, inside the closet. Where could it be?

"Did you lose something?"

She spun around and saw James standing in the bedroom doorway. She half-expected him to be holding the knife in his hand, but his hands were buried in the pockets of his robe.

She scrambled to her feet. "An earring."

"Do you want to talk about tomorrow?"

"There's nothing to talk about. How many times do I have to tell you that I'm fine?" She turned away. She needed him to leave so that she could keep searching for the knife.

James came up behind her and wrapped his arms around her tight enough so that she couldn't move. It hurt a little but not enough.

"You won't find what you're looking for," he whispered.

She tensed.

"I don't care what happens tomorrow. I don't care whether you're called Amelia or Ava or something else entirely. To me you are 'beloved' 'my heart' 'my love' and nothing will change that. I won't force you to come to me, but I'm here when you're ready." He released her.

Ava closed her eyes and listened to his footsteps walk away before she heard the soft click as the door closed.

He knew. He knew about the knife yet he hadn't said anything. How had he known? She thought she'd been so careful. He'd known and yet he hadn't scolded her. Hadn't berated her. He loved her instead.

Tears stung her eyes. She loved him too, but she couldn't turn to him right now. She had to get through this stage of her life on her own. She had to prove to herself that she could endure.

THE BEAUTIFUL ONES.

If she were to paint a portrait of Ava and her mother that's what she'd call it.

Desiree stared at Ava and her mother eating together on the balcony of the Fortune residence her heart racing. Her mother was smiling. Actually smiling! She'd never done that with her. She'd get a faint curve up of the lips, maybe, if she was really lucky, a grin, but never a full blown smile.

Her mother had never loved her that much. She'd failed. She'd truly failed to get her mother to see her, to see how much she loved her, how much she wanted for her. Ava had done it instead. Just by being born Ava had stolen her mother's heart first and left no room for anyone else. Desiree knew it wasn't anyone's fault, but she still wanted someone to blame. She wished she'd never been born so she wouldn't have to face this heartache. It was different for her brother. Their mother was proud of her son. Her dear son. But not her daughter. Desiree was just a poor replacement for the daughter she'd lost.

The daughter she now had again.

She turned away. She couldn't bare it anymore. The contrast between them was too stark and cruel.

But it also gave her freedom. Now she no longer had to carry the burden of her mother's sadness. Ava was the cure. At least she'd made that happen. Perhaps that was something.

Desiree picked up her grape juice then watched Ava charm Laurence. That amazed her. She finally saw how Ava had gotten James's attention. When she wasn't acting like royalty she could be very funny and sweet. Desiree watched Ava and her brother as they spoke about things she could barely understand and he looked so excited and hopeful and intrigued. He'd never looked at

Desiree that way. With her he always looked slightly bored.

She didn't belong. She didn't want to belong. She was better off alone. She'd be happier that way. All her life she'd been trying to make others happy (doting on her mother, worrying about her father, making up games and excuses for her brother when their mother let him down) now she could focus on herself.

She set her glass down, excused herself and left the happy trio.

She sat in the kitchen. No one would bother her there. She knew that Edgar was out of town and James had taken Rudy to the park to give them privacy. Desiree didn't know how long it was before her brother came looking for her. "So this is where you disappeared to. What are you doing here?"

I'm surprised you noticed I was missing. "I had to make a phone call."

"Well, now you can come back."

"In a minute."

"Ava asked about you."

"Why?"

He frowned and sat down in front of her. "Don't be like that."

"Like what?"

"She's curious about us."

"She wasn't that curious when I was around before. What did you tell her?"

"Just that you're a great sister to have."

Desiree nodded. That was sweet of him, but it didn't make her feel better. "Mom looks happy."

His brows shot up. "I know. I've never seen her like this. It's like she's a new woman."

"Yes," Desiree said trying not to sound bitter "Ava will never have to know what we've had to deal with."

Laurence was quiet for a moment then said, "You can't blame her for this."

"I'm not blaming anyone for anything."

"But you're upset."

"Doesn't matter. I just need some space."

"Mom loves us too."

Desiree shook her head, fighting against tears. "Not like this. Never like this. That doesn't bother you?"

"No, she's the mom we've got. I accept that."

"Of course you do. You're the sensible one."

"Before all this I was worried about you. You made Mom your entire focus. Now you can live your own life. Dad too."

"Right. I guess I should thank Ava for that." She stood. "I have to go somewhere."

"But—"

"Tell them I'm sorry."

And she was. Sorry that she felt this way, but she couldn't stop herself. A seething anger was growing. She walked to her car.

Live her own life. She didn't know what that was. What was a life without worry? What was a life without the hanging fear that her mother wouldn't make it through another day? This freedom was a little scary. She didn't know who she was anymore. Who was she supposed to be? She wanted to call her father, but feared he'd be just as dazzled by Ava as everyone else was. She couldn't stomach that. Not now. Not yet. She had to center herself.

It was time to rock.

CHAPTER 42

She looked like she was having a seizure. A strange, rhythmic seizure.

Max stared at Desiree as she sat in her car shaking. When he'd texted her to see how this important day was going, she'd replied that she'd wanted to sink in a hole. He didn't know if it was her sense of humor, but her text had so alarmed him that he'd raced over to the Fortune house to see what he could do. However, he hadn't expected to see her in this kind of trouble.

Scared, Max started towards her car until he felt the boom of a beat. She was listening to music and convulsing. Singing every word to some song only known to her. A violent song from the way she moved, crude, too, if he was reading her lips right.

She rested her head on the steering wheel. He wondered if he should disturb her. He knocked on the window. She jerked her head up and he saw tears in her eyes. She quickly wiped them away and opened the door.

"What is it?"

"Are you okay?"

She sniffed. "Yes. What are you doing here?"

"I came to see you." He cleared his throat. "What were you doing in your car?" He noticed it was parked at the bottom of the drive far from the house.

"You saw me?"

"Hard not to."

"I didn't think anybody would. I usually park in places where no one can see me." She sighed. "I listen to music. Not the kind of music you'd like. It helps me think. It gives me the words I can't think of myself."

"Show me."

She shook her head. "I'll scare you."

"I don't scare easily."

She looked at him for a long moment then nodded, "Get inside." Once he was seated she said, "I'm going to turn the volume down but the music will stay the same. Ready?"

He nodded.

Even with the sound turned down Max felt like he'd been hit with a sheet of ice. The wail of something dying filling the car with its screeching voice.

Desiree closed her eyes and let the music take over. It was a risk to let him, to let anyone, see her like this but she wanted to be completely free. To see if he could accept her as she was. Bruised, broken, angry. Not caring about someone else's happiness. She raged through every lyric letting it flow through her and say what she always wanted to say.

She bobbed her head feeling hot, sweaty, dirty and

alive and knew she was revealing too much and didn't care. This was the real Desiree. The one who didn't care if you liked her, if you were miserable. The one who didn't smile all the time. The one who could punch walls and drink beer and smash the empty can against her forehead. Not pretty, not elegant. Raw and a little mean.

When the song finished she hung her head, feeling exhausted.

Silence stretched between them.

She slowly lifted her gaze. She didn't care what she saw on Max's face. Judgment, horror, she was prepared for it. "Scary, right?"

"Brave I'd say. Not my kind of music, but I guess this is your jiu-jitsu."

He understood. Tears filled her eyes with relief. "Yes."

"How long have you been this angry?"

"Feels like forever. I'm not angry all the time, just—"

"I know. You don't have to explain."

"Your ears are still ringing, aren't they?"

"Not something I'm going to admit to." He sent her a look. "A hidden rocker. Never would have guessed. Since you're being honest I will too. It was a trick."

"What was a trick?"

"I trained AP to hide and then come out and jump on my chest like that."

"Why?"

He grinned. "I'm a scary guy, he helps soften my image."

"I was impressed."

His grin widened. "I know."

She glared at him. "I should be furious."

"But you're not."

"You train little dogs and I lip sync to hard rock I guess we're even."

Max shook his head. "I only look scary." He pointed at her. "You really are. Want to get away from here?"

"More than you know."

THE SHENANDOAH VALLEY proved the perfect escape. Together they sat side by side on the porch looking out at the rolling green pastures while hidden in his isolated hillside home while a touch of the coming autumn flowed through the trees.

Desiree told Max everything she'd kept locked up inside. She told him about her father's total focus on pleasing his wife, her mother's troubles, her brother's excitement about his FIRE plan and meeting Ava. "I feel awful. I'm happy for my mother and brother, but jealous too and—" She stopped, suddenly feeling uncomfortable. He hadn't said a word and she felt as if she'd been taking for hours. "What are you doing?"

Max frowned. "What do you mean?"

"Why are you looking like that?"

"Like what?"

"Intense."

"That's just my face."

"But you're just staring at me."

"I know. I'm listening to you."

She paused finally realizing the unfamiliar feeling.

Listening? He was listening to her? She was so out of practice of having someone give her their full attention that it felt weird. Was this for real? He really was listening, not in the regular way, nodding in agreement or making an acknowledging statement but quietly, completely. He made her feel as if she were the most important person in the world. The sensation felt a little heady, intoxicating. Sexy.

How could a man listening to you be sexy?

Max frowned. "Are you okay?"

"I'm fine," she said, which wasn't true, she felt a little too hot under the collar, too aware of him. But she wanted him to keep listening. She wanted him to listen to her all night long. She mentally shook herself, girlfriend get a hold of yourself. But then she looked at him again and didn't care. She didn't want to get a hold of herself. She'd bared herself with her music, she wanted to bare even more. She took his hand.

"You don't know how much this means to me," she said. "Can I see you again?" She held up her hand before he spoke. "Don't worry. Nobody would know about us. I wouldn't tell a soul. I just...you're easy to be with. I know I'm not exactly your type, but—"

"Yes."

"What?"

"I want to see you again too." He sighed. "But I don't want to just talk and hold hands. Is that all right with you?"

She kissed the back of his hand. "You want more than this?"

He nodded.

She brushed her lips against his. "And this?"

"I want much more than that."

"So I can spend the night?"

"Only if you understand what will happen if you do."

She smiled. "I'll make a dream come true."

He started to speak then his cell phone rang. He looked at the number and swore. "Damn. I have to take this." He left the porch and headed inside, minutes later he came out and said, "I'm sorry, we have to go. I—"

"It's okay. We can finish this conversation later."

CHAPTER 43

"What did you do to her?"

Jackson looked across the dinner table at his wife, bored. "What?"

"That woman from the store. What did you do to her?"

He shrugged. It had been nearly two weeks since the incident and he was pleased with the outcome, but he didn't plan to share that with Toyin. "Why would you think I did anything?"

"Her husband came by the store begging me to stop tormenting her. She tried to kill herself."

"Which proves she's unstable."

"What did you do?"

He rubbed his chin. "We let her know how precarious life can be. How jobs can be lost. How homes can be taken, how possessions can be seized and what she needed to do to avoid the police. All very legal."

"You threatened her?"

"We warned her. I let her know how lucky she was that I wasn't doing what I really wanted to do to her."

"He told me she's in the hospital. We have to go see her. Tell her that everything is okay."

"No," Jackson said, his tone turning cold, "you'll stay away. It's finished now. Everything is exactly how it's supposed to be."

But despite Jackson's words, Toyin couldn't sleep that night. She still saw the devastated expression of the woman's husband. He had a worn, hangdog expression and drooped shoulders. To think that they'd lost a child and he feared losing his wife too was too much. He was suffering and she didn't want to add to it. She had to do something. The man had given her his number and she met with him at a local coffee shop.

"My wife hasn't been the same since our son's death," he said. "It shocked us both. He was never really social. He was a quiet, shy kid. He had stacks of manga and anime DVDs. And he even subscribed to a number of channels. We were happy he had something he loved. We didn't realize how dangerous it could be."

"It's not dangerous. I wouldn't sell something I felt was dangerous to children. I know you want to place blame but that would be too simple. It's not your fault that you let him fall in love in this fantasy world or that he confused that world for reality or the artist and story-teller who made up the story. It was a tragic end to a simple story.

"Because there's always another side. I had another mother come in with her daughter who was suffering with a chronic, undiagnosed pain. She saw an anime on

TV and it took her away from her pain, she read the entire manga series and had her mother watch the anime series based on it with her. Together it was a way for them to connect. They finally found the diagnosis and discovered there's no cure, but reading mangas and graphic novels keeps her going every day. It gives her a reason to live.

"I can't imagine the pain of your loss, but trying to find meaning in his death will drive you crazy too. I don't know exactly what my husband is up to, but I will convince him to stop. However, promise me your wife will get help or else there's nothing I can do."

He nodded. "I understand."

And Toyin truly hoped he did and that they could both put this nightmare behind them.

CHAPTER 44

Max froze when he opened his front door and saw Desiree on the other side of it. It had been nearly a week since their trip to the valley. He'd sent and received a few brief texts, but didn't want to pressure her. He'd just finished an early dinner and was lazing in his bedroom when he'd heard the doorbell.

"What's wrong?" he asked her.

"Nothing's wrong."

He frowned. "Gisele isn't here."

Desiree laughed, tugged on his collar, forcing him to bend down a little, and kissed him. "Very funny. I didn't come here for her. I came here for you."

Her kiss felt light, sweet and familiar and her laughter lifted his heart. He wasn't used to someone being so freely affectionate with him. He pulled her inside and closed the door. "Do that again."

"What? Kiss you?"

"No, say you came here for me."

"I came here for you."

"Because you want—"

Desiree walked to the living room and set her handbag down on the couch. "Because I want to be with you. Is that so hard to believe?"

His gaze slid over her body. "I told you the risk you'd take coming here."

She sent him a sly grin over her shoulder. "Does that mean I get to spend the night?"

He didn't need any more coaxing. "I'll be right back." He dashed into his bedroom and quickly picked up two magazines he'd tossed on the floor as well as a well chewed toy that belonged to AP. He had turned his attention to his unmade bed when he heard laughter.

He turned and saw Desiree standing in the doorway with a wide grin. "You're messy? I wouldn't have guessed that."

He could feel his face burning. "The housekeeper—"

She walked up next to him and nudged him with her hip. "Don't blame the housekeeper. I still would have expected military precision from you."

He lifted up the bedcover. "Give me a minute and I can—"

"No need to make the bed. We're going to mess it up again anyway." She crawled on the bed, snuggled under the covers and rested her head on his pillow. "Mmmm... it's still warm and smells like you." After a few seconds she sat up, wiggled out of her jeans and said, "Are you just going to stand there or are you planning to join me?"

He took off his shirt. "Next time—"

"I don't care, Max." She tossed her jeans on the

ground, followed by her panties. "I like seeing this imperfect side of you."

He hesitated, wondering if he should pretend to fold his shirt and set it on a chair or toss it too. Desiree made the decision for him. She grabbed his shirt and threw it before she said, "First one naked gets to be on top."

He beat her managing to take off his jeans and underwear at the same time.

"I'll get you next time."

He slid in beside her, gathering her close. "I'll let you win next time."

"You won't have to," she said curling her body into his, "next time I won't wear a bra."

Max felt himself respond to her soft body pressed against him and opened the side drawer beside him. When he didn't find what he was looking for, he reached over her to open his other side drawer. His hand fumbled through various bits and bobs—pens, a notepad, gum— but he still couldn't find what he was looking for. His heart started to hammer in his chest. "Excuse me," he said then crawled over Desiree and looked inside the drawer. How could he be out of condoms? This had never happened to him before. Of all the days, of all the women, this had to happen with, it had to be her. He silently swore. He could call someone at the front desk, but how long would that take?

Desiree made a tsking sound behind him. "Messy and unprepared. What's a girl to do?"

He turned sharply to her, desperate to fix the situation. "Give me—"

"Fortunately, I was taught never to arrive at a party

without a gift." She pulled a condom out from under her pillow and waved it at him. "I had it in my jeans' pocket," she said, answering his silent question. "I hope it's not too big or too small."

Max took the condom from her and slid it on too relieved to care about her teasing. He took a deep breath. Disaster avoided. He gathered her close and trailed a series of kisses down her arm.

"You're supposed to thank me," she said.

He began to kiss her down her front. "I am thanking you."

Desiree sighed with pleasure as his tongue made a path down her ribs to her stomach. Yes, this was the kind of 'thanks' she could enjoy. She arched her body into him, his tongue felt nice but she wanted more. She wanted to feel every inch of his bare skin against hers.

His hungry mouth seemed to roam everywhere—her ears, her neck, breasts, her thighs, but she felt another sensation too. A strange one.

His body felt tense and he was trembling. Before she could say anything he whispered through clenched teeth, "You don't know how much I want to trust you."

She could feel how much he wanted to, but it also hurt a little that he didn't fully trust her. Not yet. She knew how hard it was for him to trust her. To trust anyone. She'd shared her secrets with him about her mother, her music, her fears and desires. But she knew it wasn't enough. He still had secrets. Their relationship was still too new and it was something he wanted to keep anyone from knowing.

She wondered how long she could take it without it

breaking her heart. She liked being with him. She wanted to be with him.

Would she have to prove to him that he could trust her? Would he be like her mother? Someone she had to constantly try to make happy? No, another part whispered. She knew he was trying. He'd revealed himself to her in his letter; he'd trusted her to burn the letter and not tell anyone.

It was then she realized that there was something he needed to hear. She wrapped her arms tighter around him and said, "I'm glad it was you. I'm glad I wrote that letter to you."

He lifted his head and stared at her, his gaze hopeful, but unsure. "But—"

"I was angry then. Now I feel the exact opposite of everything I said."

She felt the tension within him subside. "I'm glad it was you too," he said in a broken whisper.

She thought he would kiss her, but he didn't. She thought he'd gather her close again and continued their foreplay, but he didn't do that either. Instead he nudged open her thighs and slid inside like he belonged there. Like he was coming home, and her body responded, adjusting and tightening around him as if it had been made for him.

Heat rippled through her when she realized that it was the other way around: He was made for her. The rhythmic movement of his hard body electrified her. He was like her music, not to everyone's taste, but perfect for her. Her body began to vibrate like the string of an electric guitar. She moaned in ecstasy and whispered his name, which made him smile.

She loved to see him smile. She wanted to keep him smiling; she wanted to keep him beside her. Because it wasn't only his smiles she loved, she was falling in love with him too.

She collapsed with languid exhaustion when they were through. She could barely lift her head when Max excused himself to go to the bathroom.

She was almost half-asleep when she realized he hadn't returned. She glanced at the side clock and noticed seven minutes had passed. Was he okay?

She sat up and was about to swing her legs over the side of the bed when he came out of the bathroom and stared at her surprised. "You're still here."

"Of course I am. Where else would I be?" She yawned then patted the empty space beside her. "Come back to bed."

He rubbed his cheek looking uncertain then did. "I don't believe this," he muttered.

She lay on her side, resting her head in her hand. "Believe what?"

"I gave you enough time to escape."

She stared at him confused. "Why would I need to escape?"

"I thought you got enough of..." His voice trailed away.

"Of what?"

"Of me."

Desiree rolled her eyes in exasperation. "What is wrong with you?" She tapped his chest. "I said I wanted to be with you. Since you made no attempt to come by my place, I decided to come here instead."

"And you were. We were together." He frowned. "Do you want another—"

"Max," she said losing patience. "I don't want more sex. I don't want a room filled with flowers, or a one night stand. I like you. I want to be with you. Whether we're next to each other, on top of each other and any other position doesn't matter."

"You just like being with me," he said the words slowly as if trying to understand them.

"Yes. I want to know all about you. I want to know why you started your businesses. What you like to do on your days off? Why didn't you ever give AP a proper name?"

"Should I tell you now?"

She shrugged. "If you want."

"Okay." He nodded, looking awkward and uncomfortable. He bit his lip but he didn't speak.

Desiree frowned. "What's wrong?"

"This is strange."

"What is?"

"I'm not used to...someone asking about me without a reason."

"I have a reason." She wrapped her arms around his waist and kissed him. "I already told you what it was." She kissed his chest. "I showed you too. But in case I was too subtle and you didn't hear me the first time, I'll say it again. I like you. I'm curious about you. I want to know how you think. I want to get to know you better."

"I haven't had that happen before."

She curled up against him. "Well...you're stalling."

He took a deep breath.

"You still don't trust me?"

He shook his head. "It's not that. I'm just out of practice. I'm not used to sharing like this."

"You can start now. I'm all ears."

"Okay." He took another deep breath. "With jiu-jitsu I liked it because it scared me a little. I always liked the idea of conquering fear. Even as a child. So studying the martial arts was good for me."

"I couldn't imagine you being afraid of anything."

"I was a little afraid of my father and disappointing him."

"So you succeeded and made him proud."

"Somewhat."

"You're amazing in all your accomplishments. He must—"

"It's not enough," Max cut in. "But that's okay. I know I still have room to grow."

She couldn't imagine how much more he needed to do. To have managed what his father had built, plus creating a couple companies on his own seemed impressive to her. She hadn't managed to hold down a job longer than a year. He had drive and discipline. He cared about his sister and family; he had friends who trusted him. What more could a father want? But Max didn't seem ready to elaborate so she left it. If his father was anything like her mother then pleasing him would be a losing battle. She could understand that.

"I haven't exactly made my parent's proud," Desiree admitted. "But it was never my top goal. Actually, I didn't really have goals. The only thing that mattered to me was making people happy. When I saw someone was sad, I tried to make them laugh. I even got giggles out of my teachers. I could have lived at school, sometimes I didn't want to go home for fear...I just wanted my mother to be okay. I wanted her to be happy. That wasn't always the case and—" She stopped and shook her head she didn't want to finish this wonderful night thinking of her mother. "I'm tired." She lightly kissed him on the mouth. "Goodnight."

She closed her eyes and didn't know how long she'd slept before the sound of a phone woke her. She felt Max move beside her then heard him softly swear.

"What is it?" Desiree asked.

When he spoke, his voice was grim. "A mistake that's come back to haunt me."

CHAPTER 45

It took one look at Jackson's expression to realize she'd done something very wrong. Toyin had come home from work to see Jackson sitting in the living room, lying in wait. "You met with him behind me back."

"Who?"

"The bat woman's husband."

"I wanted to see how she was doing and explain to him—" She took a seat in front of him. "I'm sorry I didn't tell you, but I wanted to make sure he was okay."

"Oh, he's okay," Jackson said in a cold voice. "He's better than okay. He's threatening to sue."

"Sue?"

"Yes, he's claiming that you tried to blackmail him. That we've been harassing him and his wife who has an undiagnosed medical condition."

"But that's ridiculous. I didn't say anything that—"

"He said there's a recording of you telling him that his wife had to quote 'get help or else'."

"I meant that something bad could happen to her. And that's not all I said."

Jackson jumped to his feet and pointed at her, anger in his voice. "This is why you should have let me handle things. I told you it was finished. I told you to leave it alone. Things have changed now that you're married to me. You don't know how much you're a target now. You can't be a nice, kind, understanding person. Not everyone is as innocent as they seem. Do you even know if they had a son?"

Toyin stood. "No, but—"

"Do you even know if their entire story wasn't ripped from someone else's life? Maybe they meant to make money off of us the entire time."

"I really didn't mean—"

"You should have listened to me. This isn't the first time you've gotten my name dragged into trouble," he said, referring to how she'd accidentally revealed their secret marriage in Vegas.

"You're right. I'm sorry." She spun away.

"Wait, I didn't—" He stopped and softly swore. "Baby, where are you going?"

"I have to think." She opened the front door.

"The lawyers are already on it. You don't have to do anything. I didn't mean."

"I know," she said with tears shining in her eyes. "I have to go." She left before he could stop her.

~

James sent Max a long look. "Are you sure you want to do that?"

He and Jackson sat in Max's office in the MD Defense headquarters. Max sat behind an imposing black and chrome desk, like a general ready for battle as he faced the brothers. "I wouldn't tell you otherwise. You will not need lawyers."

"It's a risky move."

A cold smile touched his lips. "I like risk. And this is as much my fault as anyone's."

"Our lawyers—"

"As I said, you won't need them. If you do, I've failed. I don't plan to. I owe you." He glanced at a solemn Jackson, who sat with his chin in his hand staring out the window as the autumn afternoon brushed the city in orange. "Will he be alright?"

"Eventually."

"I said the wrong thing," Jackson said in a quiet voice. "I didn't mean to say it like that. Now she's gone."

James shook his head amused by his brother's behavior. "She's only been gone for a day."

"What if she's left me?"

"She hasn't."

Jackson sat up and looked at him. "How do you know?"

"Did she pack any clothes?"

"No, but she doesn't really care about clothes."

"Did she take off her wedding ring?"

"Maybe she'll pawn it."

"Did she take her sketches?"

Jackson paused, his mood lightened. "You're right. She wouldn't leave them."

"And she wouldn't leave you."

"You should have seen her face. Damn. I'm going to buy her something big."

"From what Ava told me she feels really bad for causing such a mess. I think she's more embarrassed than anything."

"It's not her fault. She should have talked to me."

"She will."

"How's Ava doing?" Max asked.

"Can't tell. She seems okay. Plans to go to a museum with her mother next week. She'd wanted to invite Desiree but hasn't been able to get a hold of her lately." He looked at his brother. "Have you heard anything?"

"No," Jackson said with little interest. "Probably busy with another job."

"Maybe, but I'd really like to make sure she's all right."

"I'm sure she is. She's got another family remember?" He turned to Max. "Have you heard anything?"

"Why would I?"

"Through your sister."

"Right, uh...no," he lied, "but when I talk to her I'll tell her what you said."

"Thanks."

"Why are women so complicated?" Jackson asked.

James shrugged. "One of life's imponderables."

~

"James was asking about you," Max told Desiree that night as they finished dinner together at his place. She'd surprised him with a pasta salad. He'd told her a little bit about his day, without sharing the full scope of things.

"He was?"

"Yes, said Ava's been trying to reach you."

Her smile fell. "Oh."

"Is that a problem?"

"No, I'm avoiding her. You didn't tell them I'm here, did you?"

Max grinned. "Why would I tell them that when I enjoy keeping you to myself?"

"Thank you."

"But why are you avoiding her?"

She shrugged.

"You will have to talk to her about all this at some point."

"The last time I tried to talk to her she nearly bit my head off. She's just trying to be polite for Mom's sake. She'll get over it soon."

He reached for another scoop of pasta salad. Desiree grabbed his wrist and turned it so that his palm faced up.

"Wait. What's that?"

He looked down and didn't see anything. "What?"

She pointed to a small brown spot. "What's this?"

"A bruise, I guess."

"How did you get it?"

"I don't know."

"When did you get it?"

"It just popped up recently."

She looked closer. "Has it changed shape or color?"

He shrugged. "I don't know."

"Hm..." She released his wrist. "I think you should get it checked."

"It's just a little mole. I have one behind my ear."

"I noticed that, but this is different. It's new. Please get it checked."

"You're serious."

"Very. Make an appointment right now. You can blame me. Say your girlfriend is overreacting. I don't mind."

"What do you think it is?"

"I don't know," she said, but she avoided his gaze so he knew she was lying. He wouldn't press her. "Tomorrow, I'll get Holland—"

"No, you can make an appointment today."

"But my doctor—"

"Go to your dermatologist."

"I don't have one."

"Gisele must. Make an appointment with hers."

Max narrowed his eyes. "You're joking, right?"

Desiree held out her hand. "Do you want me to call her and find out who she goes to?"

"No, I want to keep this between us." Max reluctantly pulled out his cell phone and dialed. "Yes, this is Max Duchamp," he said when the front desk answered, "I'd like to make an appointment with Dr. Kim. My girlfriend is freaking out about a mark on my palm."

She playfully kicked him and whispered, "Overreacting, I didn't say freaking out."

"Yes," he nodded to the voice on the phone. "Okay, that's fine." He disconnected. "Wow, that was fast. They have an opening this Friday."

"Good. You'd better go and not cancel."

CHAPTER 46

The guy was huge. Not big. Huge. Not because of his height or his build, although he had plenty of both, but from a sense of power. Wallace Render took a step back from his car. He'd just finished picking up some playdoh for his daughter when he'd been approached by a large, black man wearing sunglasses.

"If I have to run after you," the man warned in a deep voice, "you'll regret it. Let's walk and talk. You can even record it if you want to."

The man turned, Wallace didn't dare refuse him, and started to follow.

"What do you want?" he asked him.

"I want you to know what blackmail and threats really look like. Since you're making that false charge against my friend I thought I might as well make it real. Don't you agree?"

"I just need some money. I've got a sick mother—"

"And I've got no patience for liars. So how best should we handle this?"

"I could have you arrested."

"Before or after I break every bone in your hand? You'll be able to use it, but it will never be the same again? Is my message starting to get through?"

He cast a frantic look around the packed parking lot. People could see them, but the man didn't seem to care. "You're bluffing."

The man adjusted his sunglasses and flashed a cold smile, that made him briefly wonder if Death really did come knocking.

"You want me to drop the lawsuit? If you do, it will cost you."

Max nodded. "It will cost you more."

Wallace swallowed. "The Fortunes can afford it. What's a couple grand to them? I don't care what you do to me, the payout will be worth it."

"I know who hired you."

Wallace stopped, scared he was about to be ill.

The man looked at him with a cold smile. "Keep walking."

Wallace hurried to keep up. "It wasn't my idea."

"Tell me everything."

"THE GUY WAS EASY," Max told James and Jackson as they sat in the VIP lounge of one of Duchamp's clubs. "He laid out the entire scheme. I didn't even have to touch him."

James shook his head. "Pity."

"You could have made up a reason," Jackson said. "I would have."

"You would have made it worse. What was he after?"

"Money of course," Jackson said.

Max shook his head. "No, jealousy. That was the real reason behind the woman with the baseball bat. She was just the beginning."

"I thought things had ended with her."

"Because she wouldn't talk and with her background in theft and fraud it made sense. It was supposed to look like a simple case. But patience paid off, when I had her followed, I found out what I needed to know. She was exactly what she was supposed to be. A very disturbed individual. But she was only the tip of the iceberg. Wallace was also just another small piece in a bigger picture. The woman in charge was very clever. I almost missed her. But after some digging, I realized there was a struggling costume shop just a few doors away from New Worlds. She'd created an online web cartoon to help promote the store but couldn't gain traction. Toyin, however, was doing well. She'd hoped that she could scare Toyin enough to want to close her shop and move. The woman she'd hired to enter the store was only supposed to smash things, she wasn't supposed to hurt anyone, but she hadn't followed instructions.

"However, when the attack didn't get the response she wanted and Toyin opened the store soon after the incident and no police were involved, that's when the woman got bolder and came up with another plan. If she couldn't scare Toyin into leaving perhaps she could get money instead. That's when she hired Wallace to play the distraught husband to talk to Toyin."

Jackson sighed. "And because Toyin's so caring she fell for it."

Max nodded.

"What happens now?"

Max grinned with malice. "She goes down."

CHAPTER 47

He was in his haven.

Like a coward, Toyin had stayed away for two days before sneaking in last night so that she wouldn't have to face Jackson and woke up early so that she wouldn't have to eat with him. But after she'd emerged from her shower she'd seen the bed was empty. She knew where he would be.

Toyin spotted Jackson standing in his enormous walk-in closet, but instead of being dressed in one of his favorite robes, he only wore a towel around his waist. He stared at his shirts. She sensed he was waiting for her. His indecision was an offer—a truce. He never had a problem choosing what to wear. Clothes were one of his most important possessions and he had every day styled in advance. At times she made suggestions and he listened but he'd never needed help on where to begin before. He knew about clothes and fashion, fabric and style. But the one thing they had in common was a love of color. That's where she could equal him.

Toyin took a deep breath and said, "You're going to the office?"

He nodded.

She grabbed a pair of dark blue trousers, then reached for a dark blue shirt, she paused when she heard him clear his throat. It was a note of warning and she realized what she was doing. Too much dark, this was Jackson. He would want a dash of color. She put the dark blue shirt back and chewed on her bottom lip looking at the rainbow of color in front of her. A great opposite color would be orange. He would go for bright orange, but today she would insist on a softer shade with a hint of white.

She grabbed an orange shirt with thin horizontal blue strips. She heard him shift behind her but he didn't make a sound. Her heart lifted in victory. Now if he was going to the office, he would want another layer, she snatched a dark vest that would complement the trousers and focus one's gaze on the orange shirt without competing with it. Lastly she stared at the collection of sports jackets. Black would be safe.

But Jackson didn't like safe. Red could work but she didn't want it competing with the orange, she would choose dark blue again, he might not like it but for once he could have a look that fell together without someone staring in shock. He liked to shock. She placed the final item on the mannequin he kept nearby then bit her lip. "How about that?"

He folded his arms. "Do you expect me to go barefoot?"

She snapped her fingers, starting to enjoy herself. Socks and shoes, of course! She looked through his orderly sock drawer and hovered her hand over a dark blue pair; she heard him clear his throat and she hid a grin. Of course he wouldn't want that when he was already wearing so much blue. She picked up a fierce orange pair that would catch more attention than his polished brown shoes. She looked at the complete outfit, pleased. He would look good in it. She turned to him. "Well?"

"Not bad." He grabbed the trousers.

"What would you change?"

"Nothing."

"You're really going to wear this?"

"Yep."

She felt oddly touched. Tears filled her eyes. She had caused him so much trouble and it wasn't the first time. She'd accused him of treating her like a child, but she'd done the same. She hadn't taken into account his true concerns, his real worry. He hadn't overreacted, he wasn't being a dramatist, he saw a real threat and she'd ignored it. Him. Now, not just him, but all the Fortunes had to bear the weight of her mistake.

He might have had a problem with choosing bad women in the past, but she also had a checkered past when it came to the people she trusted. Those she shouldn't have. She'd nearly lost everything because of trusting the wrong business partner. And she hadn't tried to look at the current situation through his eyes. How would she have felt if someone had attacked him? Would she really have calmly stood by and let others handle everything? Sometimes she feared she'd give him a reason to regret staying married to her. That fear always lingered at uncertain times like this.

She watched him get changed. She couldn't read his expression, but she knew she'd passed one test because he'd never wear what he didn't want to.

He looked in the mirror.

"You look good," she said, rubbing her hand down his back as if smoothing wrinkles from his jacket, wanting to touch him even briefly, "but you always look good."

He tugged on his collar. "No harm in polishing the diamond."

Toyin laughed. Jackson could get away with saying outrageous statements like that and making them sound true. Her sense of fun left her when she met his dark eyes in the mirror and sadness gripped her. "I'm really sorry. I should have listened to you."

He stood quiet for a long moment then turned to her and said, "I need a hug."

"What?"

He held his arms open. "A hug."

She wrapped her arms around him and closed her eyes, inhaling his scent. "What do you need a hug for?"

"My wife hurt my feelings."

She pulled back and stared at him in mock alarm. "You're married?"

He grinned then quickly replaced it with a pained expression. "I know. I can't believe it either. Me...married."

"Do you regret it?"

He gently pushed her away and playfully hit her on the bottom. "Do you really have to ask me that?"

Even though it didn't hurt, she rubbed her bottom anyway, in a show of outrage. "Sometimes I wonder."

"Do you?"

"Yes, when I make mistakes like this. I'm so...embarrassed. I wanted to show you that you don't have to worry about me. That I'm capable of being a Fortune too. Instead I get beat up and conned and might cost you—" She stopped when he walked away from her and headed into her closet. It was across from his, not as big, she'd fought to make sure, but just as organized. He insisted on it. While she didn't pay as much attention to her clothes as he did, she had a special place for her different wigs. Not ordinary wigs but costume ones in the colors of silver, purple and pink, which she would wear to her store to give her a unique look and make the patrons smile. Jackson grabbed a pink wig and put it on.

"How do I look?"

"You look ridiculous."

He looked in the mirror and frowned. "You're right, the silver one is probably better."

"What are you doing?" she asked as he whisked one wig off and replaced it with another. He adjusted the wig in the mirror, making sure the fringe in the front crossed his eyes just so. He turned to her. "How about now?"

She opened her mouth to say he looked stupid, then stopped when she realized that oddly it worked on him. He had a strange alien sexiness. The wig didn't change him as much as she thought it would. For one wild moment she thought of putting on silver lipstick and eye shadow. He could be a great character for a story she had brimming in her mind. The men looked like—she shook her head. He was distracting her and she had to focus.

"You can't go to the office like that," she said.

"I don't plan to. Who am I?"

"Are you feeling unwell?"

"Just answer the question. Am I Jackson Fortune?"

"Yes."

"The wig doesn't change that?"

"Of course not."

"Then why would you think a mistake would change the fact that you're family now? You have nothing to prove. We're in this together. You and me. And even if James and Edgar don't like it, I'll always be by your side." He took off the wig.

"Thanks. Could you do me a favor?"

"What?"

"Wear that wig for me later on?"

He winked. "Just the wig?"

She nodded.

He kissed her. "You have a promise."

She threw her arms around him. "Thank you."

He grinned and hugged her back. "Are you trying to make me late?"

She drew away. "I wouldn't want you to get into anymore trouble."

He pulled her close. "Don't worry. I know how to handle trouble." And in a quiet voice she could barely hear he said, "And I'll always keep you safe."

CHAPTER 48

"Let me guess, your wife didn't leave you," James said when his brother entered his office at BioMed Solutions with a wide smile on his face. Since they both worked in different divisions within the company—Jackson, marketing; James, research and development—he knew his brother had come to his section for a specific reason and could guess what it was. "How did you lure her back?"

"I didn't have to."

"Did you tell her everything?"

"I'll tell her later."

James nodded, understanding his brother's delay. Toyin would be hurt to find out she'd had another trust betrayed. She'd talked about trying to help the costume store lady in the past. And speaking of costumes, James looked at his brother's outfit and noticed a change. "And you're sporting a new style or is that Toyin's influence?"

"How can you tell?"

"I don't need sunglasses to look at you."

Jackson looked at his brother's dark suit in dismay. "I pity you in your grey little world."

"It's where most sane people live. Safe to assume all is well again?"

"Yes, you?"

James turned his attention to his computer screen.

"Do you want my advice?"

"Did you hear me ask for it?"

"Stop worrying about Ava. Give her a reason to worry about you."

"Again, not needed."

Jackson shrugged. "Just putting it out there as an option." He placed his palm on the desk. "She's taking you for granted. Maybe you should make her jealous. Show special interest in her sister and—" He ducked when his brother crumpled up paper and threw it at him. "Fine, I'm leaving. It was just an idea."

After his brother had gone, James pinched the bridge of his nose. It wasn't the idea that annoyed him; it was the thought that he was tempted to do it. He was tempted to show Ava that there were other women who would want a man like him by their side. He wasn't weak. They wouldn't hate his touch or his caring words.

But he also knew what that would do to her. She *expected* him to hurt her somehow and he promised he'd never do that no matter how much she hurt him. He hadn't mentioned the knife. Never wanted to.

At least now she wasn't as tense as in the past. Her

mother had accepted her. It was what she truly needed. Her fears had been put to rest, but she still hadn't turned to him. She kept a barrier up and he didn't know how to reach her.

Sometimes he feared he never would.

AVA CLOSED her latest manga with a sigh and looked up at James as he worked on his laptop. They both sat in the great room but hadn't spoken. They'd been speaking less and less these past several months. She knew most of it was her fault. She wanted to change that.

"How did everything go today?" He'd shared with her what Max had found out about Toyin's attacker and the fight she and Jackson had had.

He kept his gaze on the screen. "Jackson's in a good mood, Rudy got a brief text from Desiree that made him happy so everything is fine."

The mention of Desiree's name made Ava remember her words, warning Ava not to be too hard on James.

She looked at him. Really looked at him and finally saw what she'd refused to see.

She saw sadness. He hid it well. He was good at hiding things, but she saw he was hurting. Through everything—Desiree's initial lie, Max's anger, Toyin's attack, Jackson's frustration, even her distance, he'd had no one to turn to. She remembered Desiree's words and felt ashamed of herself. She hadn't told him anything specific about her trips with her mother. She hadn't told him how ordinary her mother had seemed. She'd made a myth of her in her mind. She hadn't told him that when her mother had cried and held her she felt all her fears disappear. That she felt a little foolish for fearing the reunion so much. She knew he wanted to hear all this. She hadn't realized how much she was hurting him by not telling him. By shutting him out.

"Mom and I went out to lunch today." The word 'Mom' got caught in her throat but she managed to get the word out even though it still felt strange.

He paused, waiting, hopeful. "Good."

She bit her lip. "Can I tell you about it?"

She saw his shoulders relax. He turned to her. "I'd like that."

She sat down beside him and told him everything and watched the sadness slowly slip from his features. She remembered that he was Flo's son and she'd been given the privilege of spending her life with him and that meant turning to him not pushing him away.

"I'm sorry," she said.

"I understand."

"I didn't mean what I said about you. I was scared and angry because of how much you affect me. How much I really care about you and how much you care about me."

"I know."

"At times I don't know why."

He lightly bit the loop of her ear and growled. "Can I show you?"

She grinned. "Maybe. Will it hurt?"

"Do you want it to?"

"Just a little." She hesitated, remembering their last fight when she'd wanted him to be more brutal with her than he felt comfortable with. "Is that okay?"

He grinned and answered her without uttering a word.

CHAPTER 49

"What's wrong with you?"

"Me?" Desiree asked, surprised by her brother's question. "Nothing, why?" She stood in her kitchen icing cookies she'd made for the "Sweet Treats" series of jewelry designs Rudy had been working on. He'd loaned her some of them and she planned to surprise him with photos of the different earrings, necklaces and bracelets with desserts as the backdrop. She felt the new images would work great on his website and help the series stand out. She'd already finished several photos of the jewelry with cupcakes and now was on to the cookies.

"You haven't dropped by my place in weeks," her brother said. "Mom says you haven't answered any of her calls. That's not like you. The moment Mom sneezes you're buying flu medicine."

She set her icing down and picked up a pair of earrings displayed in a green box. "I don't have to worry about her anymore. I've been busy celebrating my freedom."

"Sounds to me like you're running away."

She set the earrings in the center of the cookies then set the plate on her dining table. "I'm too grown for that."

"Then why haven't you shown up to any of the dinners we've had with Ava? This one restaurant she took us to was amazing. She let me take two orders home. Can you believe that?"

She put the cell phone down and put it on speaker. Sure, it's great, she wanted to say, but didn't. "There's no need. Besides, there's plenty of time for her to get to know us all. We don't need to force these meetings."

"They're not forced, they're fun and you'd realize that if you'd come."

Desiree sat down and stared at the cookies and earrings, annoyed. It would be hard to concentrate on her photography while talking to him. "I already know all I need to about her."

"She's nicer than she looks."

Good for her. "Have you told her about your FIRE plan yet?"

"I will in time."

"She's got the money. I'm sure she's got lots of brilliant ideas that can help you. Much better than the stupid ones I had." She picked up one of the cookies and bit into it. Her special job with Rudy was over, and although she'd been paid well (very well) she'd need to start job hunting again.

"They weren't stupid."

"Just not great."

"You're worrying me now."

"There's nothing to worry about. Really. I'm fine. I'll talk to you later."

"How about we get together? Just the two of us? You wouldn't believe who I've been seeing."

Laurence sounded so excited and happy. She was happy for him. Her throat closed. He was seeing someone, which was rare. Had Ava given him the confidence to get out of his shell? She loved him but she still hated him a little bit for liking Ava so much. She didn't want to see him until she had her feelings under control. "Another time. Bye." She disconnected before he could reply. It was better this way. Ava had probably charmed her father as well and then...then the replacement would be complete. Because that's how it felt. That she had been a stand-in all her life. That her mother had been waiting for her true daughter to return, that her brother was waiting for the big sister he could really relate to. And her father? He'd want anyone who could make his wife smile. In Ava he would have found that person.

There was no room for her. And she didn't want to feel like an extra tire. She was now free to live a new life. A life away from her mother's sadness.

There was no one she had to try to please. It made her feel a little lost. It had been her role and identity for so long. But now she could find out who she truly was.

LAURENCE PUT AWAY his cell phone then rejoined his parents at the dinner table. It wasn't the same without

Desiree. Ava had come over to his parents' house once, and the meal had been nice, and his parents happy, and he'd tried his best to keep the mood upbeat, but the place felt a little empty without her.

"Did you get a hold of her?" his mother asked.

"She's fine, just busy."

"She's never been this busy before."

"I'm sure you'll hear back in a week or two," his father said.

"But—"

His father covered her hand. "It's a lot to adjust to. Give her time."

"I only hope she's all right."

"She's a big girl. She knows how to take care of herself."

His mother nodded, pleased. "Yes, she always has."

Laurence didn't want to admit how much he wished they worried about her more. He didn't want to admit how much he missed her. How much he wanted to hear about her latest exploits. He also wanted to tell her about his new relationship. It had happened faster than he could have imagined and his new girlfriend didn't want anyone to know about it yet, but he wanted to tell Desiree.

He knew she could keep the secret for him. But he also had to stand on his own. He'd left her to deal with their mother's moods for long enough. She had a right to take a break from them. He hoped it wouldn't be too long.

CHAPTER 50

He felt foolish about going to the doctor for something so small. Max sat in the private lounge of the dermatologist's office and sighed. He couldn't imagine why a little mark would bother Desiree so much, but if this silly visit would put her at ease, he didn't mind.

But the doctor surprised him. She asked him a series of questions about the mark (asking him how long he's had it, if it had ever been painful, itchy or bleeding) she examined its size, texture and color before she checked out the rest of his body looking for other moles and spots. She felt his lymph nodes and then took a digital photo of the spot on his palm.

She sighed and sat back in her chair after looking at the photo for a long moment. "I'm glad your girlfriend had you come in."

"Why?"

"It's melanoma."

He couldn't believe his ears. "Melanoma. You mean skin cancer?"

She nodded. "Yes."

"How can I have skin cancer?"

"Anybody can get skin cancer. Too often blacks ignore small symptoms like this and feel that skin cancer doesn't affect them. But it does and, more often than not, because of finding out too late, or waiting too long to get a strange mole checked, the cancer has a chance to spread and ends up being fatal. You're a classic case. For blacks, melanoma usually shows up on the soles of the feet, your legs, bottom, palms, or private parts. I want to take a skin biopsy. Whatever the tests show, I believe we've caught the cancer in time to be aggressive enough to take care of it. I'm glad you listened to her. If it is a squamous cell carcinoma, which can spread to the lymph nodes and organs we'll..."

The doctor's voice faded into the background. He couldn't hear the rest. He didn't want to hear strange words and think about radiation, surgery or other forms of treatment. Cancer? *Skin* cancer? Him? A man as brown as a walnut? He couldn't wrap his mind around it. He'd gone to the dermatologist to not worry Desiree, but a diagnosis like this... How could he tell her? Should he tell her? Was this something their relationship could survive? What if she saw him in a new way?

He barely felt the tiny sting of a needle as the doctor gave him a local anesthetic. She removed the mole and told him it'd be sent to the lab.

Max left the office in a daze. He was walking absently to his car when his cell phone alerted him to a text.

Desiree: How was it?

He couldn't tell her, not yet. She was still dealing with the stress of her mother and the realization she had a sister.

Max: Just a little mole. They removed it in the office. I might have scar.

Desiree: So, everything's fine?

Max stared at the screen for a long time not knowing how to respond. No, it's not fine. I've got cancer. They're testing it now to confirm the diagnosis and see if it's spread. He briefly closed his eyes. No, he couldn't tell her that. He wouldn't tell her anything.

Desiree: Max?

He thought of the monster house. He thought of the monster house because he wondered if that was how his body would become. Despite how he'd cared for it, would it become dilapidated and worn, broken down, leaving him as the tired, lonely old man inside waiting for death? For the first time in a long time he was truly scared. He didn't want to be alone. He didn't want to lose her.

Max: Yes. It's fine.

She sent back the image of a kiss and a heart. Max looked at the image of the heart feeling as if his own was breaking.

CHAPTER 51

That night he held her close as they lay in bed together. Over dinner she'd beamed with pride that he'd gone to the dermatologist and told him how relieved she was that everything was fine. She then told him about how much Rudy had liked her photographs and when James had seen them he'd offered to pay her for them. When they'd put them on the website, Toyin had been so impressed by her work she wanted Desiree to take some pictures of items in her shop she wanted to sell online. She had told him how happy she was that the Fortunes would keep her busy so that she didn't have to look for another job yet. She even considered taking another course in photography to improve her skill. He was happy for her. Twice, he'd thought of telling her the truth, but didn't want to remove her smile. He told her he had something he'd tell her later.

Max closed his eyes, the warmth of her body the only solace he had.

Desiree snuggled closer to him. She wasn't asleep. She was too happy to sleep. Finally her life seemed to be working. When she'd seen the tiny Band-Aid on Max's palm, where the mole used to be, she'd felt her heart lift. She'd initially been nervous about it, but now there was nothing to fear. Also, the Fortunes had really liked her photographs, they'd called her creative and clever.

She had a man she cared about, work she enjoyed and now she felt confident enough to spend time with her mother again, Ava too. It was time to stop running away. She wondered what Max had to tell her, his tone seemed odd, but she wouldn't worry about it too much. Things were looking up for them. Desiree sighed and started to drift off to sleep when her cell phone rang. She quickly grabbed it not wanting to wake Max.

"Hello?"

"She took everything," Laurence said near tears.

Desiree paused. She'd never heard her brother sound like that before. "Who? What did she take?"

"My new girlfriend. I thought she really loved me. Now my FIRE fund is gone. So is she. I don't know what I'm going to do."

His tone alarmed her. She sat up. "Where are you?"

"I'm at home. Although I'm not sure how long I'll get to stay here."

"Wait for me. Better yet keep talking to me, I'm coming over."

"No point," he said dejected. "There's nothing you can do."

"That's not true. You know me. I always come up with a plan. Tell me who she is."

"She's your friend Rachelle. I've been seeing her for a couple months."

Rachelle! Oh no! Desiree closed her eyes and groaned.

"Desiree," Max said, placing a gentle hand on her shoulder. "What's wrong?"

"Laurence hold on for a second, okay?" She turned to him and muted the phone. "It's my brother. I have to go see. He's saying Rachelle conned him out of his money."

"Rachelle? Rachelle Weaver?"

She nodded. "I introduced them before I knew the truth about her and I didn't tell anyone else about her."

Max swore then jumped out of bed. "I'll drive you."

She wanted to say no, but knew she wouldn't be able to focus on driving. "Thanks." She took the mute off and spoke to Laurence "...are you still there? We'll be right over."

"No, I only called to say goodbye."

"Don't talk like that. I'm on my way."

Although Laurence initially protested, Desiree kept him talking, hardly understanding most of what he said, until they were at his door. Desiree rushed inside his apartment and saw him laying on the couch looking broken and despondent.

Then she saw the gun in his hand.

She paused. "Laurence. It's going to be okay."

He stared at Max with wide eyes, terrified. "Who the hell are you?"

"He's a friend of mine and he wants to help."

"Nobody can help me."

Desiree held out her hand. "Give me the gun."

He shook his head. "I have nothing to live for. A stupid loser like me doesn't deserve to live."

"This hurts, but you'll recover and—"

"I'm sorry, Desiree." Laurence lifted the gun. But before he could lift it to his head and pull the trigger, with one swift kick Max knocked the gun from his hand and grabbed it. Desiree had been so distracted by her brother that she hadn't noticed Max moving closer to him until it was over.

Max emptied the gun chamber. "I know how you feel," he said, placing the bullets in his pocket.

Laurence hung his head. "All my plans are ruined."

Desiree rushed over and hugged him. "You'll stay with me tonight. You're going to be okay."

She felt guilty. The feeling seized and squeezed her. If she hadn't kept her distance from him she would have heard what he was doing with Rachelle. She could have warned him. If she had listened and stayed in touch she would have told him the kind of woman she'd found out Rachelle was, without betraying Max's secret. She should have been more careful when she'd introduced them, she'd even encouraged Rachelle to go after Laurence and break him out of his shell.

This was all her fault. He'd been trusting. She'd called Rachelle a friend. And she'd taken that trust and she'd used her brother. Used her.

Her jealousy of Ava had blinded her to the special relationship she had with him. So she couldn't talk about science or economics, but he was always eager to hear her advice about being with people. It was an area he was always lacking even as a child. She helped him to learn which friends were mean (no it's not right that you have to buy DJ a chocolate bar every day) versus true friends (yes, it's okay to split your ice cream with her since she invited you over to play). She loved being his big sister and their well-meaning teasing. She'd missed that. How awful she had been, taking what they'd had away from him.

She hugged him tight, fighting tears. "I'm so sorry. I'll make this up to you."

She tucked him into bed, as she used to do when he was a child, then stood over her bed and watched him sleeping. It had taken nearly an hour to get him to calm down enough to rest.

She left her bedroom and walked into the living room then stopped when she saw Max sitting on the couch watching something on her flat screen TV, which seemed the size of a napkin compared to the size he was used to. Everything about her place seemed smaller. He'd never been to her apartment before and it was like seeing a Great Dane relaxing in a bed made for a teacup poodle—adorable and ridiculous. She'd forgotten he was still there and felt a little ashamed of her worn furniture and pile of unfolded clothes on her coffee table. "I'm sorry to drag you into this."

Max shook his head, his tone grim. "You haven't done anything. How is he?"

"Sleeping for now."

"What do you plan to do?"

"I still can't understand everything, but from what I can piece together Laurence fell for a classic investment scam. Rachelle promised him she could double his money. I hope to get the full story from him later."

"How much do you think she took?"

"Close to a hundred and fifty thousand. I know that might not seem a lot to you, but it was carefully crafted and—"

"You don't have to explain. I know for a guy of twenty-eight that's an accomplishment. I also know it's not only about the money."

"No."

He stood. "I have to go."

She didn't want him to go yet. "You said there was something you wanted to tell me?"

"It can wait. This is more important." He lightly touched her arm. "Take care of yourself. I'll be in touch."

"Right," she said, watching him leave. He seemed distant, cooler towards her. He hadn't even offered her a brief kiss, instead he'd patted her arm like a relative.

He probably wanted nothing more to do with them. Drama seemed to follow her. Rachelle! How could Rachelle have popped up in their lives again? She didn't blame him for wanting to run away. She wanted to do the same from this crazy life of hers. A mother who married a man who'd stolen her child, a woman who lied to impress strangers, and then a brother who got swindled by a charming woman? Max wouldn't want to tie himself to a woman like that. He'd dealt with enough pain, he didn't need more.

They'd kept their relationship a secret. Was this the end for them? The thought hurt, but she couldn't be angry at him. It was all her doing. Her pettiness with her brother had caused a rift that never should have happened.

And there was no one to tell. She didn't want to shame her brother by sharing a private moment: That he'd been so despondent that she'd found him in his usually clean apartment, with items broken and things in disarray with a gun in his hand. She didn't want to hear any callus remarks such as 'if he'd really wanted to kill himself, he would have pulled the trigger' the incident would be something only three people would ever know.

But what would she do now?

She fell on the couch and cried.

The following morning she woke up to find a note Laurence had left saying he'd taken vacation time and needed time away, but that he wouldn't do anything to hurt her. He didn't want her to worry or tell their parents about anything that had happened.

She tried to reach him, feeling anxious, but when her calls instantly went to voice mail she realized she didn't have to deal with this on her own. She had someone who could help her. Family that could help her. She called Ava.

"I'm sorry to bother you," she said. "But...it's Laurence."

"What's wrong?"

"He's disappeared and although he says he's taken vacation time I'm worried about him because it's not like him. I don't know what to do. Is there a way you can help me?"

"Of course. Come right over."

She didn't tell the Fortunes the entire story just that Laurence had been upset and then she showed them the note he'd left.

James put a reassuring hand on her shoulder. "Don't worry. You don't have to deal with this alone."

CHAPTER 53

*R*achelle Weaver had gumption.

Max hated the woman but he couldn't help being impressed. He wasn't surprised to see her sipping champagne wearing a gold silk gown in the suite of a New York City luxury hotel. On the table sat a bowl of fruit and expensive chocolates. The one thing she knew how to do well was spend money.

To her credit, she didn't look surprised to see him. She didn't ask how he'd gotten inside her room or why he was there. Instead she smiled. "Max, what a surprise."

He sat down in front of her.

"Why Desiree Foster?" he asked in no mood for small talk. He knew that Rachelle didn't approach anyone without a reason.

She didn't misunderstand him. "I spotted her on the college campus with Rudy Fortune."

"And you saw an opportunity?"

She shrugged as if the answer was clear. "When I saw

her at the gastro bar, I thought why not?" She sipped her champagne. "I thought I'd get close to the Fortunes, but then she changed for some reason and I realized I'd have to look for another...friend." She smiled. "You know I'm adaptable."

He also knew when she used the word 'friend' she meant 'target'. "So you went after her brother?"

She grabbed a red grape and ate it. "He's young with a good job. He'll make his money back and more."

Max bit back his anger at her callousness. She'd left Laurence devastated with a gun in his hand, wanting to end his life. "True. I know you'll likely wiggle out of a conviction on identity or credit card fraud, but what about computer fraud?"

She frowned. "Computer fraud?"

"Yes, you got too greedy. That was your biggest mistake."

She took another sip of her champagne showing little interest. "I don't know what you're talking about."

"I managed to notice that you accessed his bank account to transfer even more funds to the fake investment scheme you persuaded him to join. That's different than adding an extra zero to a cheque you deposit into a personal account. It's a more serious infraction too."

Her expression changed to alarm. "Max—"

He stroked his chin, pensive. He enjoyed her unease. "Let's see...computer fraud is a serious crime. You could be found guilty of a felony and face twenty years in jail."

She slowly set her wine glass down. "What do you want?"

Max folded his arms.

"If you take me down, it will hurt you too. I know things about the Duchamps you wouldn't want anyone to know. Like Gisele's surgery."

He grinned amused. "Are you threatening me?"

Rachelle hesitated as if unnerved by his expression. "No, you're a businessman, let's come to a compromise."

Max waited.

"I'll get some of his money back and—" She stopped when she heard a knock on the door.

"No, what you're going to do is surrender to the police, but that's only the beginning because I plan to make you regret that you ever crossed my path." He stood. "Goodbye Rachelle."

CHAPTER 54

*D*esiree never expected all her fears could disappear within five days. But they did when her brother called her sounding like he used to. She sat in her apartment, scrolling through a collection of photos on her laptop when the call came.

"I figured out a way to recover some of my money," he said, "and even though it will take a little longer than planned I can still work on my FIRE plan."

She sighed relieved. "I'm so glad."

He hesitated. "Sorry I scared you like that."

"Sorry I wasn't there for you."

He fell quiet again then said, "But you still saved the day. I don't know how they found me, but they saved me."

"They who?"

"Forget it. Nobody. I wasn't supposed to say anything."

"Who?" she insisted.

"You know James and that other guy."

"Max?"

"Yeah, Max. He stopped me from doing something bad. I wasn't going to kill myself, but I was about to try to make money in a way I shouldn't."

James and Max had been there? They'd found him? She hadn't heard from Max in a while, except for a couple of texts telling her he was still out of town on business. But she knew James was back and James would be the one to tell her the full story. She called to say that she needed to see him and asked if they could meet at his office. Instead he invited her to the house and welcomed her into the great room with a smile.

"What's going on?" he said.

"I need to know something."

He leaned back in his chair. "Go on."

"Did you and Max help my brother?"

James shook his head before he smiled and said, "Looks like Laurence can't keep a secret any better than Rudy can."

"Tell me what happened."

"I don't think—"

"If you don't, I'll bug you for days. And if that doesn't work I'll go to Ava and—"

James held up a hand in surrender. "Okay, you win. What do you want to know?"

"Everything."

"You're right. We were involved in finding your brother, but Max did most of the effort. He said he felt the most responsible because he knew what kind of woman Rachelle was. He asked me to use some contacts to locate your brother, and after that he took care of the rest. Your brother was about to make a deal with some dangerous and shady people, Max was able to put an end to that in a way that made sure your brother wouldn't be approached again. He convinced him to come with us and also helped me come up with a way to offer him some contractual work that will help him recover financially. Max put a stop to all the credit cards Rachelle had set up in Laurence's name and put out an alert. So your brother is safe."

"What about Rachelle? What if she—?"

"Max found her in New York and now she's facing federal charges."

"I can't believe he'd do all that."

"Then you don't really know him. I told you months ago that you'd seen him at his worse. He's not the cold, cruel man as some people like to paint him. I wouldn't be friends with someone like that. In time perhaps you'll see that too."

Since James didn't know about her relationship with Max she couldn't let him know the truth about how differently she felt about Max now. "Perhaps. Do you know when he'll be back in town?"

"Tomorrow, I heard. Are you going to talk to him?"

"Yes. I think I should thank him."

James groaned. "I was afraid of that. Tell him that you tortured me first before I told you everything. I have a reputation."

Desiree smiled. "Of course."

She said her goodbyes and headed for the front door

when she saw Ava coming down the stairs. She picked up her paced.

"You don't have to keep avoiding me," Ava said, "I'm not going to press a relationship on you that you don't want."

Desiree stopped and turned. "It's not that. Thanks for all you did helping Laurence."

Ava nodded and folded her arms. "But that's not what you really want to say to me."

She was too smart. Desiree sighed. "I stayed away because I envied you."

Ava stared at her surprised. "Envied me?"

"Why do you sound so surprised? It can't be the first time in your life that people envied you. When you won an award at sixteen, started and ran a successful company, married a great guy."

Ava sniffed. "I also had a father who hardly complimented anything I did. For years I thought my mother had abandoned me because I wasn't good enough. I've worked hard for everything I've got not sure I'd ever make anybody proud."

She'd never thought of that. She'd never taken the time to think about what kind of childhood Ava had lived. "I'm sorry."

Ava nodded. "I'm sorry too." She paused before she said in a quiet voice, "From what Laurence told me, it's been really hard for you too. We both didn't come out of this ugly past unscarred. I'm happy with the life I have now. I'm grateful that I got to meet my mother and start anew with her. But what scared me the most was the thought that I'd have to be someone else.

"I realized that I don't. That I have people in my life who accept me as I am and that means everything." She took a deep breath. "I guess what I'm trying to say is...you're amazing. I like you. I may not show it the way others do, but I do. If we hadn't been related, I'd want to know you anyway. I know why James wanted you to be Rudy's companion. Jackson and Toyin think you're great. The light you've brought into our lives has been incredible and if our mother can't see that then she's blind."

Desiree felt tears in her eyes. She hadn't realized how much she'd wanted someone—anyone—to say that to her. To see the hard work she'd done and recognize it. She hadn't thought that someone like Ava would have noticed her effort, but the fact that she did amazed her.

"I'd be so lucky to have a daughter like you," Ava continued, "but I think having a sister like you is incredible too. And we're all so happy you're part of our lives now—"

Desiree reached out and hugged her. All the bitterness, anger, jealousy left her and all she saw in front of her was a woman she could love. A woman she *did* love. A sister who understood her pain and was willing to share it. Her mother may not be able to love her the way she'd hoped, but she now also had James, Rudy, Jackson, and Toyin. She belonged and they were happy to know her. She wasn't alone. She was appreciated. She felt loved in return.

She knew she startled Ava and steeled herself to be pushed away, but Ava didn't. She hugged her back and whispered, "I'm sorry Mom hurt you," and then they both cried.

Desiree drove home feeling renewed. She couldn't wait to see Max and thank him. But when she entered her apartment and received a strange call from Gisele everything changed.

"Did you know Max went to see my dermatologist?" Gisele asked her confused.

Desiree hesitated. She knew his visit wasn't something Max wanted his sister to know. "Yes, I asked him to, but it was nothing."

"I'm not sure about that. Dr. Kim said he missed an important appointment, but she wouldn't tell me more than that. Just encouraged me to get him to go see her. Do you know what that's about?"

"No." But she planned to find out.

CHAPTER 55

Max wiped his face with a towel as he left his studio. He'd had a good workout, but he still felt on edge. He'd returned to town two days ago, getting James to lie for him, but he knew he'd have to face Desiree eventually. He wasn't sure how yet.

But when he left his studio and saw her standing there, he knew that time was now. He couldn't read her face, which was rare. That's what he loved about her, she was easy to read. But she stood in the hallway with a guarded expression.

"Is something wrong?"

"I have to talk to you."

He inwardly groaned. That was never good. "Let me take a shower first."

"Fine."

The fact that she hadn't argued made him feel worse. What was going on? Back in his apartment Max quickly showered then changed and met her in the living room where she was rubbing AP's stomach.

He sat down in front of her. "Okay, what is it?"

"I have to thank you."

"For what?"

"What you did for my brother."

His jaw twitched.

"Don't get mad, Laurence couldn't help himself, but he only told me a little. I got the full story from James."

His brows shot up. "I'm going to—"

Desiree waved his annoyance away. "I threatened to torture him. I said horrible things."

He folded his arms.

"I don't know how we'll repay you."

"You don't have to. I didn't want to see another victim of Rachelle's lies not get justice. Plus, I'm partially responsible. If I hadn't told you to keep what I'd said a secret you could have warned him."

"That's true," she said slowly. "But I think you're keeping something else secret from me too."

He stiffened. Had she found out he'd come back to town early too. "What?"

"Dr. Kim asked Gisele why you missed an appointment. Why would you need to see the doctor again if everything's fine?"

Max stared at her, stark, vivid fear gripping him. Not only was his lie about to be exposed she wanted to learn the truth.

Her voice shook. "Everything isn't fine, is it?"

He swallowed hard and shook his head. He looked at the ground and said in a low voice, "I'm sorry."

He heard her move then felt her sit down beside him, but he couldn't look at her.

"Why do you have to see the doctor again?"

He looked at the scar on his palm. "It wasn't a mole. The doctor says it's cancer. The skin biopsy said it wasn't benign."

"Why did you lie to me?"

"I didn't want to worry you."

"Has it spread?"

He shook his head. "I don't know."

"What happens now?"

"More tests, some treatments, I guess. I was supposed to talk to her about it."

"You should have told me. Why did you miss your appointment?"

"Because your brother's more important. I had to do something. I told you it was my fault and I know how much he means to you."

"Without knowing how much you mean to me?"

He turned to her surprised. "What?"

"How could you think I'd want you to sacrifice yourself for my brother? Why would you think I'd want to choose? I asked you to see the dermatologist because I was worried about you. I care about you. Bob Marley died from melanoma. Most blacks don't know how deadly skin cancer can be to us."

Max shook his head. "You shouldn't have to go through this with me."

"And you shouldn't have to go through this alone." She took his hand. "Not when you have someone willing to stand by you."

Except for his sister no one close had cared about him like this.

He felt healthy and strong, how could this invader have entered his body? When had he let his defenses down? What had he done wrong? His father had said he was weak. Was this proof?

"You can't control everything," Desiree said as if reading his thoughts. "We'll deal with this together." She held him close. "You saved my brother. Your kindness saved me as well."

He hesitated. "I did it for you."

She rested her head on his shoulder. "If I were to write you a letter right now, this is what I'd say: My darling Max—"

"Darling?"

"Yes, because that's how I think of you. Now be quiet." She cleared her throat. "My darling Max, I know you might be scared right now. But you're not alone. I hoped I'd convinced you of that when I wrote you that letter all those years ago. When your sister told me about you, I felt as if I'd met a kindred spirit. Someone I'd want to have by my side. I still feel that way now. You're the one person I never felt I had to make happy. Being with you is enough. I will always be there for you. Yours Desiree."

"And I'd say: My dear Desiree—"

"Not 'darling'?"

"No, it would start: My dear Desiree, I'm sorry I ever hurt you. Until I met you I never knew the angry and bitter man I had become. I'd done to you what I wished I'd done to Rachelle, publicly humiliating her. I'd become arrogant and self-righteous until I realized you were the one who'd written me that letter all those years ago. Words I'd memorized."

She lifted her head pleased. "Really?"

"Yes, shut up. I'm not finished."

"Okay."

"I memorized every word. You showed me a side of myself I didn't want to see. You shook me up and then you changed me. I'm glad you're in my life. Max."

Desiree wiped away a tear. "That's a beautiful letter."

He kissed her then whispered. "And I mean every word."

CHAPTER 56

He wasn't a man she dare refuse.

The phone call from Max's father had been completely unexpected. As was his request to see her. He told her a driver would come to pick her up and didn't give her a chance to decline. She was still over the moon that Max had treasured her letter to him and that he'd gone to the doctor and learned that the cancer hadn't spread. With treatment he would be okay. She wasn't going to lose him, but getting a call from his father worried her. She put on her best outfit, blush pink wide leg trousers and white satin blouse, all the time wondering what he had to say to her.

When she entered the VIP lounge of the Duchamp club she faced her greatest fear. A nightmare. A monster. She looked at Mr. Duchamp and saw a man who'd given his son his imposing build and piercing dark stare, but none of his tenderness. She saw someone she could never please. Someone who would never like or accept her. Mr.

Duchamp represented every colleague who'd ruined her lunch, spread rumors behind her back, and tried to make her life miserable.

Except she couldn't run away. Her relationship with Max wasn't a job she could quit. She could be fired, but she wouldn't leave on her own. No one would run her away. It wasn't only Max's happiness on the line but her own.

"You're exactly the type he would fall for to spite me," Mr. Duchamp said giving Desiree the once over. "No degree—"

"I have an associate's degree."

"No, degree," Mr. Duchamp said as if proving his point. " You've barely kept a job, have a brother who gets himself into trouble. Don't look so surprised. I like to keep my eye on things from a distance. You chose a very good target. I had to meet the young woman determined to ruin my son's life."

She knew he meant to insult her, but she wouldn't take it that way. "Yes, I do plan to ruin it. I plan to ruin a life spent in fear. Fear of being betrayed, fear of failing, fear of being abandoned. I want him to live a life where he's not afraid to trust someone. Where he knows someone has his back just because they care."

"You live in a very simple world."

"People complicate it with lies."

"One of the biggest lies my father told me was work hard and you'll be rewarded. That by being a good man you'll gain respect. My father was a fool as was his father before him. In my youth I helped a local club owner get new clients. I busted my ass off and what did he do? Gave it to his son. That's when I knew I'd been taught to play a sucker's game and had to look out for myself. Next time I didn't help a struggling business I took it and another after that. Nothing was given to me. I didn't get to where I am today by being nice and working hard. I worked smart. That's what separates the winners and the losers.

"You don't know what you'll do to his reputation. Not only will no one of any importance want to be around you, you will secretly be laughed at. Everyone will know the true reason you married my son despite your pretty smile and charming personality. It will wear thin eventually. When you're ostracize and—"

"The world is bigger than your small circle. If I have a future with Max it will be far away from anything you can imagine. It will not be based on return on investments or dividends. It will be based on things that are immeasurable like joy, compassion, generosity."

"You need money to be generous."

"I find that the rich don't seem to be as generous as they claim to be. If you're here to threaten to disinherit him, that you'll punish him for staying with me, I accept that. I won't accept you insulting me or my family. You don't know me; I know you don't care to try, so save your breath. You can't scare me away. Not this time."

"This time?"

"Before I met Max being liked, making people happy was the most important thing in the world to me. But it secretly made me miserable. Now I don't care. I'll love your son whether you like me or not. I'll stay by his side as long as he wants me to. That's all I have to say."

"Fine words but my son isn't as strong as you think.

He lacks the conviction to defy me. Not a second time. He made a mistake with a woman before and she fleeced him. He thinks I don't know the truth, but I found out. He was too proud to admit he'd been fooled he let people believe she'd left him. As if getting thrown over by a woman like that was better," he sniffed in disgust. "You won't last. When he realizes that you're truly worlds apart. That you can never get him what he truly wants, you'll be disappointed. I'm trying to save you from heartbreak."

"I can take heartbreak. Your son—"

His voice turned cold. "Don't lecture me about my son. I know his fears, I know his desires. I've built him from the ground up. I made him. Literally and figuratively. He owes me. He knows that and he knows the choice he has to make."

When he left, Desiree collapsed on the couch, feeling exhausted. She knew she wouldn't change his mind about her, but it still felt like a battle and she wasn't sure she'd won. He was right. What future could she hope with Max? Only his family knew about their relationship. He'd wanted to keep it secret. She'd never attended any of the events he went to. What if she did embarrass him? What if he did grow tired of her?

Did he love her enough to face life together? Did he love her at all? Was she just a diversion? Was she asking too much?

She wiped away tears.

"No, don't do that."

She glanced up and saw Max.

"Don't let him make you cry."

She flashed a watery smile. "How did you know I was here?"

"You'll soon find out that the Duchamps like to keep an eye on each other. Someone at the club let me know you were here."

She wiped another tear away.

He handed her a tissue. "I told you not to cry."

"I'm not crying because of him. It's you."

He knelt down and looked up at her. "I made you cry?"

"No. I just...I don't want you to be ashamed of me."

"I've never been ashamed of you."

"I don't have a university degree."

Max shrugged. "Neither does he and I don't mind being seen with him."

"But you didn't want anyone to know about us."

"I never said that either."

"But we never did anything public."

"Because I liked keeping you to myself. I wasn't joking about that."

"I want this to last."

A slow smile spread on his face. He pulled a ring out of his pocket, "If you're asking me to marry you," he slid the ring on her finger, "the answer is yes."

She gasped. Not at the sight of the stunningly unique ring or even his beautiful smile. What made her gasp was how much he loved her and how much she loved him in return. How much she wanted to spend the rest of her life with him. Her heart filled with joy and she wrapped her arms around him and teasingly replied, "I knew you would say that." She drew away and looked down at the ring, which was made up of two twisted sterling silver rings sandwiching a gold band. "This is very distinctive."

"I asked Rudy to design it for me. I thought it was fitting since he's the one who brought us together."

Rudy! She finally got to wear his ring without any regret. She'd wear it forever. "Thank you."

He kissed her before he said, "No, thank you. You finally helped me to understand something."

"What?"

"When I was a little boy I met my grandfather and he looked like this pathetic old man in this scary looking house and my father always scared me by telling me that I'd end up like him if I didn't do what I was told. It was later that I learned that my grandfather had worked most of his life as a machinist in a paper factory. He never made a lot of money, but lived his life with pride. When I'd met him most of his friends had passed as well as his dear wife, but, later, when I was older, I learned those who had known him always spoke about him with respect. He didn't have my father's status, but he also didn't have his anger and loneliness.

That day I realize he tried to save me when he whispered to me: *I don't know much and I don't have much, but I've always had joy and been rich in love.*

A YEAR LATER...

At their wedding reception Max stood at the head table and announced, "Everyone I have a confession to make."

James and Jackson shared an uneasy look. Desiree felt her heart pick up pace. She'd heard those words before and what had followed hadn't been good. Although she was surrounded by friends and family, the absence of Max's father was evident and his mother looked far from pleased.

"Desiree will you please stand?"

She briefly looked at Ava for help, but she just shrugged her shoulders. Rudy smiled at her with encouragement while beside him sat his new girlfriend, someone he had met at the recreation center, who'd always liked him. A quick glance at Laurence returned a blank expression as did Gisele. Nobody knew what he was up to. She took a deep breath then stood.

Max gestured to her. "I have never nor will I ever love anyone as much as I love this woman. She frustrated me and challenged me, but best of all, she made me a better man." He raised his glass to her and smiled. "And I'll never be the same."

The crowd cheered.

And Jackson glanced at Toyin while James smiled at Ava, who would welcome their first child in a few months, before the brothers held their wine glasses up to Max in a silent gesture of understanding. For the three men knew that the love of a woman had saved them all.